RE-IMAGINING THE CHRISTMAS TRUCE

RE-IMAGINING THE CHRISTMAS TRUCE

Peter Riach

© Peter Riach, 2021

Published by Peter Riach

All rights reserved. No part of this book may be reproduced, adapted, stored in a retrieval system or transmitted by any means, electronic, mechanical, photocopying, or otherwise without the prior written permission of the author.

The rights of Peter Riach to be identified as the author of this work have been asserted in accordance with the Copyright, Designs and Patents Act 1988.

A CIP catalogue record for this book is available from the British Library.

ISBN 978-1-9989948-0-9

Book layout and cover design by Clare Brayshaw

Cover image Illustration © Naddiya | Dreamstime.com

Prepared and printed by:

York Publishing Services Ltd
64 Hallfield Road
Layerthorpe
York YO31 7ZQ

Tel: 01904 431213

Website: www.yps-publishing.co.uk

Contents

1	Prelude to War and Truce	1
2	The Negotiations	23
3	Reaction to Peace Terms	44
4	Progress on Peace	57
5	The Wedding	66
6	Consequences of Peace	76
7	The Iron and Steel Community	95
8	Consequences of Peace in Australia	98
9	1925	104
10	Celebrations	113
	Addendum – 1929	137

Chapter One

Prelude to War and Truce

RORY Hunter flew above the pack of players in black and white jumpers and grabbed the oval ball. He then walked back slowly and deliberately and kicked the ball between the two high goalposts. The boundary umpire collected the ball and raced it back to the centre circle so the field umpire could bounce the ball to resume play. Before he got there the siren sounded to indicate close of play, which meant that Richmond had beaten their old rivals, Collingwood, to win the Championship. Rory was the Richmond captain and he was lifted high by his team and paraded around the ground in triumph.

When they returned to the changing room in very high spirits the Vice Captain, Ken Stanley, asked if there was any intention to respond to the recruiting drive aimed at supporting Britain and France in the battle against Germany. It was early September in Melbourne and the current belief was that the war would be over by Christmas. "If so" said Ken "we'll back in time for the next football season." There was some minor grumbling but it soon subsided when it was pointed out that they would be in France and French sheilas were reputed to be quite forthcoming.

After they had showered and dressed the whole team set off for the recruiting office. The recruiting officer immediately recognised them and Rory explained that the only condition attached to their volunteering was that they all be combined in the one fighting unit. This was not a problem and the recruiting officer said that it would make obvious sense for Rory to be the Sergeant and Ken to be his Corporal. In two days time they were to report for intensive training in trench warfare.

The evening did not go so smoothly, for whereas they had expected a jubilant time celebrating their Championship success, they faced outrage from wives, fiancées and girlfriends. Their men were going off to the other side of the world to face a serious danger of death. Some of them had also heard the rumours about French women so they considered that they faced a dual danger. Rory was engaged to Lorraine and she was particularly upset as they had planned to marry in the New Year.

A recruiting officer was setting up his stall in the cloisters of the University of Melbourne. He was approached by a young man who indicated he was keen to volunteer. He explained that he was studying modern European history so he had some understanding of the historical animosity amongst European countries. He was also studying the German language and had a respectable level of fluency in the language. This was music to the recruiter's ears and he suggested that he would be a good candidate to be a junior officer. He enquired about the young man's hobbies and interests. He explained that he was a very keen footballer and played in the centre for the University team. "Excellent" said the recruiter. "We have just signed up the Richmond football team with Rory Hunter as the sergeant and I think you would be an appropriate second lieutenant. How do you feel about that?" "I am a Carlton supporter myself but I do admire the skill of the Richmond players so it would be an honour to be associated with them." Thus Samuel Harcourt was dispatched to the training ground to unite with his new army mates.

They were trained in how to use a rifle and the various aspects of trench warfare including over-running an enemy trench and collecting valuable information. They also learnt how to clear a village which they had over-run, but there was no need to work on their physical fitness, as their football training had meant they were in top physical condition.

Before they were shipped off to Europe they were addressed by Colonel Monash. He explained that by profession he was a civil engineer but had long been a member of the University of Melbourne's part-time militia. Now that war had been declared he had become a full-time soldier and was to be the officer in charge of the Fourth Infantry Brigade. His philosophy of warfare was for the infantry to have maximum support from artillery, mortars and aeroplanes and never to advance unprotected into no-mans land where they were likely to be cut down by remorseless machine-gun fire. He believed in doing all he could to safeguard the welfare of his men. Monash was the son of German Jewish immigrants so there had been some public opposition to his appointment as an officer in charge, but what he had just said gave reassurance to the recruits who intended to pass it on to their womenfolk before they departed for Europe.

The wives, fiancées and girlfriends did take solace from what Monash had said, but nevertheless some still considered that they faced the dual risk of death and infidelity. Lorraine had made up her mind to confront

Rory. "I want us to make love before you go just in case you don't come back." "Oh I can't do that" said Rory "what if you got pregnant and I did die; you would be an unmarried mother and I'd have fathered a child I would never see: a child without a father." "But you know I am very regular and it's not possible to get pregnant two days before your period is due, so there is no risk involved." Rory did not need any further persuasion.

12,000 miles away in a Lancashire town called Accrington the mill workers were discussing their response to a poster calling for volunteers to join the fight against a German army which had almost overrun Paris. "It says that if we join up as a group we will be kept together during the fighting." "Conscription is certain to come soon, so it may be sensible to be seen as volunteers and be kept together so that will be able to support each other." Graham Blakey's father had been a Chartist so his son had inherited his radical disposition and was the natural political leader of the Accrington mill workers. They emerged from the recruiting station reassured that they would be combined as a fighting unit with Graham Blakey as their sergeant.

Hundreds of miles north in the Speyside region of the Highlands the distillery workers had gathered in Rothes to discuss their response to Lord Kitchener's recruiting drive. "Why should we get involved fighting alongside Sassenachs who have treated us badly over centuries" said Kenneth MacNamara. "But we would be fighting alongside the French in defence of their country and you must remember the auld alliance, which existed for centuries and which meant that the French came to our aid whenever we had a dispute with the English. I would be proud to honour our historical links in the memory of Bonnie Prince Charlie" was the response of Angus

MacDonald. "I understand that French women are curious about what we wear under our kilts, so I would be more than happy to inform them" added Fergus Buchanan. So off they went to join the Northern Highland brigade and came out wearing their newly acquired kilts and with Angus McDonald as their Sergeant.

The German advance was rapid and they reached the outskirts of Paris before they were finally driven back by taxi-borne French infantry. The Germans were then pushed north by the British and French allies in the "Race to the Sea". The "Accrington Pals" and the "Northern Highlanders" joined the British Expeditionary Force in a Belgian town called Ypres. Throughout November they experienced vicious trench warfare and suffered significant casualties.

Meanwhile Australian and New Zealand volunteers had been travelling by ship to England. On board they had been undertaking vigorous physical training so that they would be battle-ready on arrival, but they did have spare time and Rory and Ken decided that they should take advantage of Samuel Harcourt's knowledge to learn the history of conflict between major European powers. Rory explained that the only European history they had been taught was about Henry the Eighth and his various wives, and about Elizabeth the First and the Spanish Armada. Samuel Harcourt was happy to oblige and added that he could also teach some basic German if any of them were interested.

Samuel explained that the English and French had been fighting each other off and on for centuries, and that in the 14th and 15th centuries there had been something called the Hundred Years War. Just over a century ago there had been something called the Peninsula War, which had pitted Portugal, Spain and Britain against France. This culminated in 1815 in the Battle of Waterloo in which the Duke of Wellington's Army, with the critical support of the Prussians, defeated Napoleon. What we now know as Germany had not been founded until 1871 under the aegis of the Prussian, Bismarck. Between 1870 and 1871 there had been the Franco German War which had resulted in a humiliating defeat for the French and the annexation of Alsace and about a quarter of Lorraine, which included valuable iron ore deposits, by the Germans.

"As the English have been fighting the French for centuries and the Prussians were their key ally in defeating the French at Waterloo, why are the roles now reversed with the French as the English ally and the Germans as the enemy?" asked Rory. "That's a very sensible question" replied Samuel, "so I will now need to explain to you the convoluted origins of this war we are now in."

First you need to be aware that Queen Victoria had a large number of offspring, who were married off into most of the protestant royal families of Europe, and even a granddaughter who was Queen of Catholic Spain. George the Fifth of Great Britain, Kaiser Wilhelm the Second of Germany, and Tzar Nicholas the Second of Russia were all grandsons of Queen Victoria and therefore cousins. The interconnections were confirmed by the fact that the Kaiser was an Admiral in the Royal Navy and George the Fifth was Colonel of the Prussian first guard dragoons. Only France and Switzerland of the European countries were not monarchies. You presumably know of the bloodbath which accompanied the removal of the French Monarchy.

There were five major European powers at the turn of the century: Britain, France, Germany, Russia and Austria-Hungary. The British navy dominated the sea but the

Germans were hell-bent on achieving naval equality with the British, whilst the French were extending conscription with the intent of achieving military equality with the Germans. The ruling class of Austria-Hungary was dominated by Germans and Magyars, but their empire included the Slav people of the Balkans. Slav resentment at this had led to war in the Balkans in 1912 and 1913. Austria, France, Germany and Russia all imposed conscription for two years on young men, after which they joined a reserve army for several years.

Several treaties of military cooperation had been negotiated during the latter part of the 19th century. In 1890 Germany and Russia agreed that Russia would be neutral with Germany, unless the Germans attacked France and that Germany would be neutral with Russia, unless it attacked Austria-Hungary. In 1892 a Franco-Russian convention agreed that both countries would mobilise and jointly go to war if either were attacked by Germany. Belgium's neutrality had been guaranteed early in the 19th century by an agreement between the British and the French and the Prussians. By early this century the British and French had agreed that if Germany violated this agreement British soldiers would cross the channel to fight alongside the French. So you can see that these treaties, negotiated within the belligerent background of the European powers, were set up, like a set of dominoes, to achieve a continental-wide war.

The spark which ignited this war was the assassination of the Archduke of Austria in Bosnia by a Serb nationalist in June this year. In retaliation a month later Austria-Hungary declared war on Serbia. So it followed that Germany came to the assistance of Austria-Hungary and that Russia came to the assistance of Serbia. Next, in August, Germany declared war on France and demanded that Belgium allow German troops to use its territory in the fight against France. Germany refused the British demand that German action against Belgium should cease. This meant that early in August Britain, France and Russia were all at war with Germany. "So that briefly explains how Europe came to be in this highly bellicose state of affairs" said Samuel.

Next Peter Wood, a Richmond winger noted for his speed and currently an economics student at the University of Melbourne, said "I might not know European history but I do know a lot of Australian history, so what I want to know is why we are involved in this continental war 12,000 miles away, which is amongst these countries who have been squabbling amongst each other for centuries." "It's all about 'home' or the 'old country'; in other words Britain: and Australia being part of the British Empire" explained Bob Fraser who was a Richmond backman. "But don't you know that Australia was established as a dumping ground for English criminals, most of whom had committed petty crimes, and who were treated as white slaves on the journey to Australia and on their arrival in Sydney in 1788. My great grandfather was a convict on that first fleet and I know of his suffering including being flogged. His crime had been to steal some items of clothing in London: a crime which nowadays would incur only a minor prison sentence" replied Peter. "The last time we went to the assistance of the 'old country' in a war was in South Africa and I'm not sure we received many thanks for that, and moreover the British executed one of our men called Morant in controversial circumstances."

"I would add that many thousands of Irish were amongst the convicts who were transported to Australia, and that in the middle of the last century many thousands more fled

Ireland to Australia to escape the potato famine; many of my forebears were amongst them" said Paddy Guinness, who was a robust Richmond forward. "The English invaded and fought to take over Ireland during the 16th century; the land was confiscated and handed to absentee English landlords who treated their Irish tenant farmers harshly. Throughout the last century the Irish struggled to achieve home-rule, so I agree with Peter that there is little logic in us participating on the side of Britain and France in this brawl between European powers." At this stage Samuel Harcourt intervened, "I do understand what you're saying, but remember we all signed up to serve in this war and to be loyal to George the Fifth. We have to accept this for the duration of the war, but when you return home you would have the right to agitate for independence, as the Americans did in the eighteenth century, and if successful, to leave the British Empire and replace an English aristocrat Governor General with an elected Australian President. You could do this by either joining one of the established political parties and pursuing your cause within it or by establishing a new Republican Party."

In November the Australian troops joined the British in the trenches at Ypres. They were stationed alongside the Accrington Pals and the Northern Highlanders. Donald Bruce, who was a Richmond Rover and the son of a Scotsman, explained the tradition of Scottish soldiers wearing kilts. He added that teasing them about wearing female clothes, or about what they might wear under them would be something they would do at their own peril.

The Australian troops began to experience the mud of the trenches and the terror of machine-guns in no mans land. They were commanded by an English captain who was a stickler for regulations and military protocol. One morning, after they had been in the trenches for a week, he announced that, on the orders of military headquarters, they were to climb out of their trench and cross no mans land in order to drive the Germans out of their trenches and push them north. When the appointed hour came he indicated to them that it was time to climb out of the trench and proceed across no mans land to fight the Germans and drive them out. Rory pointed out that he had not seen or heard any artillery shells land in the German trenches or in no mans land, so how could he order them out into no mans land unprotected to face a barrage of machine-gun fire. Captain Berkeley said it was now the time which had been ordered by military command for the advance "so get to it immediately!" "But where is the covering Artillery" shouted Rory. "Oh they always miscalculate the range and the shells would've landed behind the German front-line" shouted one of the Accrington Pals. "This is not what we signed up for and you're a bloody fool", Rory shouted at Captain Berkeley as he climbed, with his teammates, out into no mans land. "You'll be on a charge if you come back" was Berkeley's reply. Machine-gun fire began as soon as they emerged, so they scrambled into a large shell hole, except for Alan Wright who was their leading ruck man. He was tall and well built, but slower than the others, so he had been hit in the legs and head by machine-gun fire.

The teammates cowered in their shell hole in a mixture of sadness and fury as they mourned the loss of their teammate. They scrambled out when darkness descended and retrieved their teammate's body to take back to the trench. Rory immediately set out to find Captain Berkeley: "you bloody murderous mongrel". "Be very careful, you're already on a charge" replied Berkeley. "You're the one who needs to be careful as I'm going to have great difficulty restraining my teammates from lynching you". "That's it, I'm calling the military police immediately" was Berkeley's response. "You'd better call for a whole contingent of them because there are 20 of us, and I don't doubt that the Northern Highlanders will join in our defence." At military headquarters they received an urgent phone call telling them that Australian troops had mutinied and were threatening the lives of officers. So a large body of military police were needed to arrest them and take them into custody.

Fortunately Monash was present and intervened to say that, whatever was going on, sending in a large quantity of military police would only inflame the situation. He emphasised that he was their commanding officer so he would go to investigate the situation, and if there was any decision to involve the military police it would be one which would be taken by him, not some English Captain. When he arrived at the Australian trench he asked for Samuel Harcourt and requested an explanation of what had been going on. Samuel explained that they had been ordered to go into no mans land unprotected by the artillery fire he had promised. Consequently they had immediately encountered machine-gun fire and Alan Wright had been killed. Rory had challenged Captain Berkeley about the order to proceed without artillery assistance, but had been ordered with his comrades into no mans land, consequently it was perfectly understandable that he had reprimanded Captain Berkeley. Colonel Monash then went immediately to interrogate Captain Berkeley and asked him why he had so negligently risked his men's lives by ordering them into no mans land without artillery support. He replied that he had been strictly following the order from military headquarters to attack at a particular time. "Did it not occur to you to check what was happening with artillery before proceeding?" asked Monash. Berkeley replied that at the Royal Military College he had been trained to obey orders unlike this rabble of Australians. "I had given these men an undertaking that they would not be exposed to danger in no mans land unless they had adequate artillery support, so they were relying on their commanding officer's assurance, I am promoting Lieutenant Harcourt to Captain and transferring you to headquarters in the hope that you will do less harm there".

Monash then called all the Australian troops together and explained what he had done, and that when he got back to headquarters he would insist that it must be understood that no English Major could overrule Samuel without his express permission. When he returned to headquarters, the Generals, who were all Royal Military College men, were outraged that this part-time, German Jewish soldier had taken such action. Monash explained to them that it would be pointless trying to have him removed, as he did have the support of the Australian Prime Minister and he intended to contact Louise Mack and give her precise details of what had just happened. This would mean that the entire Australian public would be aware of the reckless action, perpetrated by an English officer, which had unnecessarily put Australian lives at risk. He was aware that there was in Australia a pacifist movement led by a woman called Vida Goldstein, which was very active and this would inevitably lead to a demand for Australian soldiers to be repatriated. He was also aware that there was a Melbourne suburb where Berkeley would be burnt in effigy.

When it appeared, Louise Mack's Report had an immediate impact nationwide. To the Irish catholic community it simply confirmed their belief in the perfidy of the English military. Back in the trenches the Richmond players continued to lament the death of their friend and teammate. Ken Stanley articulated what they were all thinking "What we were told was wrong. This war obviously is not going to be over by Christmas and I very much doubt if it will be over by the following Christmas. No-man's land is a death trap for both us and the Jerrys. I'm sure they must be just as pissed-off with this miserable and dangerous battle as we are."

On Christmas Eve they heard across no mans land "Stille nacht, heilige nacht, alles schlaft ... einsam wacht...." "What's that?" said several of the Richmond players in unison. "They're singing Silent Night which is a German Christmas carol" said Samuel. "We don't have any Australian Christmas carols, but when they've finished why don't we sing Waltzing Matilda in return?" said Rory, so later 20 voices rang out "Once a jolly swagman camped by a billabong under the shade of a coolabah tree....." When they finished a German voice called out "What's that, we don't recognise it?" "It's an Australian folk song" came the reply.

"Mein Gott! Are there Australians over there? We know of your reputation in the South African war. It's bad enough having to face the "Women from hell" but now we know you Australians are also over there. No wonder we've been getting such a hard time". "Would you agree to meeting in no mans land tomorrow to exchange presents and drink some wine together? There is no reason why this wretched war should cancel our normal Christmas festivities." Samuel quickly consulted Rory and then shouted back "Jawohl wir werden kommen". Rory quickly informed the troops and they scurried off to the nearby village to buy some "plonk" for the celebrations.

Just after sunrise both sides hoisted a white flag and crossed into no mans land. They shook hands all round and pooled their resources of French and German wine to be drunk later in the day. They exchanged cigarettes, cigars and chocolate and the Germans contributed some schnapps to the drinks pool. Some of the Germans were keen to hear of current progress in the English football league. When it was discovered that Samuel Harcourt was a student of European history he was asked to provide a quick outline to the Germans, whose own education had been very partial. They was surprised to hear that their Kaiser was a cousin of the Russian Czar and the British king: two countries with whom they were at war. They also wondered why the British were fighting against them alongside the French when a century ago the Prussians had been a key British ally in the war against Napoleon. Most of all, they wondered what the Australians were doing here 12,000 miles from home when their own country was not being threatened. It was discussed amongst all groups involved and it was concluded that inept statesmen on all sides were responsible for this wretched war which had developed into stalemate and attrition. So their thoughts inevitably turned to the extent to which they had been consulted by these war-makers. The Australian, Belgian, French and German troops all had had the right to vote for their current lawmakers, but British men were restricted by a property qualification, which meant that many of the Accrington Pals and Northern Highlanders had had no right to vote for a government which had sent them off to war. The Australians were very surprised to hear that no European country allowed women the right to vote in national elections. Women had been granted the right to vote in Australia in 1902, just after the federal government has been established in 1901 and prior to that the colony of South Australia had extended the vote to women in 1894.

Samuel Harcourt explained that currently in Britain there was a movement of women called suffragettes who had established a party called the Women's Social and Political Union and were dedicated to achieving full voting equality for women. They were quite militant and when their demands were rejected they took to tactics such as disrupting Parliamentary proceedings, setting fire to postboxes, smashing the windows of shops, chaining themselves to railings and even setting off bombs. When they were imprisoned they went on hunger strike and had to be force-fed in a very cruel way. Last year a woman called Emily Davison had thrown herself under the King's horse at the Epsom Derby and died as a result. The leader of the suffragettes was a woman called Emmeline Pankhurst. There had been a famous philosopher/political economist called John Stuart Mill who had been a strong advocate of women's suffrage last century. He had written a book called the Subjection of Women, and in1866, when a member of Parliament, he attempted to amend the Second Reform Bill to extend the franchise to women. He failed but it triggered an ongoing debate about the enfranchisement of women.

Graham Blakey emerged with a soccer ball. "Enough of these politics. I grew up with this, as my father was a Chartist involved in the campaign for male suffrage. Now it is time for some fun and some friendly, non-lethal competition between the British and the Germans". They crudely marked out a pitch and laid down piles of entrenching tools to serve as the goals. The Australians looked on as the Accrington Pals and Northern Highlanders fought with the Germans over the ball without the use of their hands. The problem was that no man's land was littered with potholes caused by the interminable fighting. This meant that it was impossible to control the ball, which could fly off at unintended directions. Rory ran back to his trench and collected an oval ball. "It will be easier if we play Australian football, which is rather like Irish football. The idea is that you kick this football high in the air and as far as possible, and then your team and your opponents try to catch it, and if one is successful they are allowed to stand back and kick it rather like a freekick in soccer. There is no need to kick it along the ground so we wouldn't have the problem which you are currently having with the soccerball. If you agree we can teach you how to play this afternoon and then tomorrow we can organise the match. I'm sure no one would disagree about extending this truce for another day."

The Richmond players organised themselves into two teams and played a robust game. The British and Germans noted a lot of body contact, which would not be permissible in soccer and were very impressed with the distance the football could be kicked especially by Paddy Guinness.

Rory handed the oval ball to Graham Blakey and the British and Germans proceeded to have a kickabout and, in particular, to get used to catching the ball. Rory arranged that half the Richmond team would join up with the British and the other half would join up with the Germans in tomorrow's match. He got the Richmond team together to explain that they should be careful not to dominate proceedings but allow their European teammates to have a good share of the action. It was getting dark so they repaired to the German trench, which was more robustly and comfortably constructed than the British one. They shared German bratwurst and French cheese while setting about demolishing the wine. When the wine started to run low Fergus Buchanan offered to go back to the French village and purchase some more. He took the opportunity to engage with the young lady behind the bar who was serving him, but was quickly chased off by her mother, who was herself an elegant French madame. She explained that she had heard rumours about Scotsmen's kilts and perhaps he would like to come upstairs and confirm what she had heard. He was happy to oblige and consequently did not get back to the German trench until the wine was about to run out. After much jollity they wished each other a happy Christmas/Weihnacht and the British set off to their own trench promising to be back in the morning for the football match.

Over the Boxing Day breakfast both the British and the Germans chose who would be in their teams and it had been agreed that there could be plenty of substitutes so that as many as possible would be able to test their skill at Australian football. Fergus Buchanan declined to participate and again volunteered to buy the wine. He felt he had more exciting prospects for the day.

The Richmond players agreed that whilst they would bump each other vigorously as usual, they would go easy on the British and Germans who were not accustomed to such physical contact in soccer. The game proceeded with great enthusiasm and Ken Stanley, who had volunteered to be umpire, was kept busy explaining what was and what was not permissible in the way of physical contact. Both sides scored several goals, but what most impressed the Richmond players was a German called Hans Schmidt. He was tall and most adept at jumping high over the pack of players to catch the ball. This included out-marking several Richmond players. The game finished with a close victory for the Richmond/German team and it was agreed all round that it had been a great success and that it would be good to play again tomorrow to give the Richmond/British team a chance to avenge their defeat; anything to delay returning to this internecine war.

Over lunch Rory spoke to Hans Schmidt, with the help of Samuel Harcourt as translator, and asked if, after this dreadful war was over, he would be interested in emigrating to Australia and playing with the Richmond team. Hans said that he had very much enjoyed the game and he would give it some serious thought and come up with some relevant questions for Rory.

Next Rory and Samuel spoke together privately. "Did you notice that, after you explained recent European history and the origins of this conflict, the Germans were just as bemused as us that we are here fighting each other in this way?" said Rory. "Yes" said Samuel "so what I intend to do is approach the Germans and ask if an officer and sergeant would like to join us for a discussion after lunch."

Most German officers spoke reasonable English and they checked around for a sergeant who also spoke English, so that the four of them could all communicate in English. The German officer was Fritz Prowse and his sergeant was Wilhelm Muller. As everyone else was having a post-lunch glass of schnapps in the German trench, the four of them set off to the British trench for a private discussion. Samuel explained that they had noted the German curiosity and concern about the origins of this war, which is now compounded by the fact that we soldiers obviously enjoy each other's company and obviously would find it difficult now to go back to shooting each other. "I certainly could not imagine shooting Hans Schmidt" said Rory. "I agree, but what are we to do?" said Fritz. "We should press for an armistice so that there can be discussions about resolving this dispute by peaceful means without this needless slaughter of many thousands of lives" was Samuel's response. "Richtig" said Fritz "I suggest that we return to our respective trenches to discuss this proposal for an armistice and how we should proceed. Then we can come together over an evening meal and some wine to agree a course of action."

The British and Australian contingent were unanimous and enthusiastic in their support for an armistice. When they came together with their German adversaries they found an equivalent level of support for an armistice. Consequently, after they had eaten, Samuel, Rory, Fritz and Wilhelm got together to discuss how they should proceed. They had heard that there had been many Christmas truces along the front line, so it was agreed that they should try to move speedily eastward along the front line to advocate the case for an armistice, while there may be fertile ground for a positive response. Fighting alongside the British to their right were the French, and as Angus McDonald's mother was French he was fluent in the language and he was added to the negotiating team. Fritz also had a reasonable command of French so the five-man team moved east to explain the proposal for an armistice to their respective comrades. Some of the French were unenthusiastic because of the grievance they had over the Germans snatching Alsace and part of Lorraine last century. Samuel and Fritz assured them that this would be the principal concern during the armistice negotiations. So the French were reassured and agreed to support agitation for an armistice. Pierre Girardin, who was a lieutenant and spoke good German, was added to what was now a six-man team.

They moved east and explained the rationale for an armistice and found most soldiers on both sides in support, especially when it was explained that the Alsace-Lorraine problem would be the number one issue on the agenda of the proposed armistice negotiations. They did encounter the occasional soldier who dissented. In particular there was a German Corporal who kept ranting on about Jews and how they were subverting German society." "I'm Jewish" said Samuel Harcourt "and so is Colonel Monash who is our commanding officer and dedicated to taking care of his troops and minimising casualties." "This is the type of evil prejudice which led Simon de Montfort to chase Jews out of Britain in the 13th century and which led to the pogroms in Russia last century. You should try to keep this Corporal isolated so that he does not infect other troops. Perhaps you could have a Jewish officer keep him under control."

The captains and majors who were present on the front line had initially been relaxed about the informal Christmas day truce, as they realised the soldiers had had a very grim time at Ypres, but now that they got wind of this tripartite quest for an armistice they became very nervous about the reaction to be expected from staff headquarters behind the lines. As the senior Australian officer, Colonel Monash was called in at headquarters to be reprimanded. "We believe that you Australians and, in particular Lieutenant Harcourt and Sergeant Hunter, have been instrumental in this 'mutiny' so we have it in mind to send in the military police to arrest them." "I would strongly advise against that", replied Monash. "I am their commanding officer and I must remind you of the controversy in Australia about British judicial proceedings against Australians in the South African war." "Also it is not a 'mutiny', as they have not refused to fight, but instead, with their German opponents, conducting a truce and attempting to resolve this European dispute by getting agreement to an armistice and negotiation. If they are able to resolve this dispute satisfactorily in this way it will save tens, if not hundreds, of thousands of lives. You will not be amongst these casualties, so how can you deny them this opportunity to achieve a peaceful outcome. You must know the satirical song which they sing about you with great gusto. "One staff officer jumped right over another staff officer's back and another staff officer jumped right over that other staff officer's back – they were only playing leapfrog – I predict that you will all be the butt of much satire in future years." They grumbled a response and clearly many of them were not impressed by this argument. Monash finally added "Have you forgotten, or ignored, that I promoted Lieutenant Harcourt who is now Captain Harcourt?"

Samuel and Fritz had envisaged a response of military police action, and it was agreed that the six of them would have a bodyguard to protect them against the military police. The plan was that a large group of German soldiers would protect Samuel, Rory, Angus and Pierre, whilst a large group of British soldiers would protect Fritz and Wilhelm. This meant that there could be no allegation of insurrection. When the British MPs did turn up to arrest Samuel and Rory, expecting it to be a simple task, they were confronted with a large number of German soldiers who explained that they had no desire to hurt them, but that they would defend John and Rory to the death if challenged. The German MPs who arrived to arrest Fritz and Wilhelm faced British troops who also explained that they were peaceful unless forced to protect Fritz and Wilhelm. Both sets of MPs retreated to headquarters to report the situation.

The band of six proceeded southeast along the front to Belfort and the Swiss border. The word had spread about them and in general they were enthusiastically welcomed, although there were always a handful of dissenters; one young French lieutenant called De Gaulle was amongst the most outspoken. Nevertheless the vast majority on both sides supported this quest for an armistice and the possibility of a peaceful solution to the dispute. When they passed through Nancy they were impressed by its elegance and decided that it would be a very appropriate place for the armistice negotiations. After completing their discussions with the troops in the Belfort area they set off back northwest, explaining as they went that they would now negotiate with the various governments involved how the armistice negotiations would proceed and how the participants would be selected. En route they encountered the German officer who had been in charge of the rabid anti-Jewish corporal. "Did you have much trouble with him?" asked Samuel. "Massive" was the reply "he just wouldn't shut up and was determined to subvert the quest for an armistice." "So what did you do?" "I shot him." "Oh golly" said Samuel, "given what happened to Breaker Morant during the South African war we better take immediate action. Where is the body so we can take it into no mans land and make sure that it looks like he was killed in action?" They found a nearby shell hole which had several German bodies in it, dumped the body amongst them and threw in a couple of grenades. "That should do it" said Samuel, "for the record what was his name?" "Hitler" was the reply.

Chapter Two

The Negotiations

PIERRE said that they would have to accept the virulently anti-German President Poincaré as a member of the French team, but he could be balanced by Jules Cambon, an experienced diplomat and negotiator, who had played a vital role in achieving the treaty between Spain and the USA in 1898. Graham and Angus conferred about the British nominees: "we propose the Chancellor of the Exchequer David Lloyd George who is a very compassionate man and the noted suffragette Emmeline Pankhurst." Because of his Chartist upbringing Graham was a strong believer in women's right to vote and he also thought that having some women on the negotiating team would be more likely to produce a peaceful outcome. Pierre was impressed by this argument and said that he would like to add the name of a very famous French woman to his suggestions. Marie Curie was a brilliant scientist who had actually won two Nobel prizes – in physics and chemistry – which was unprecedented. He was certain that someone as clever as her would see the logic of a peaceful outcome to this dispute and would be formidable at arguing her case. Samuel said he accepted that the Australian Prime Minister

Fischer would have to be included but he recommended that Fischer be balanced by Vida Goldstein. She was a suffragette and was one of the first women to stand for the Australian parliament in 1903. She was a pacifist and was involved in establishing the women's peace army, which campaigned against Australia's participation in this war. As she was also noted for being an impressive public speaker he was certain she would more than hold her own during the peace negotiations.

The Allied powers now had seven nominations including two suffragettes and Marie Curie, so it followed that the Germans needed to come up with seven nominations, of which at least one should be a woman. Fritz said that Bethmann-Hollweg, the German Chancellor, as the counterpart of Poincaré, Lloyd George and Fischer, was an obvious choice and to his credit he had been attempting to engage in peace negotiations with the British. Also the appropriate counterpart to Emmeline Pankhurst was Marie Stritt, a prominent German feminist, who was a founder and important leader of the International Women's Suffrage Alliance. Wilhelm suggested that, because the allies had nominated Marie Curie, the Germans should nominate their famous scientist, Albert Einstein. He also suggested that these two famous physicists should be complemented by the famous German sociologist Max Weber. As a counterpart to the German Chancellor Bethmann-Hollweg they chose to nominate Hugo Haase, who was a pacifist and leader of the Social Democratic party which had won 35% of the votes in the 1912 elections. As the Allies had nominated three women, Fritz and Wilhelm decided to match them by nominating Clara Zetkin and Rosa Luxemburg. Clara Zetkin had been involved in the establishment of International Women's

Day. Kaiser Wilhelm had described her as "the most dangerous witch in the German Reich". Rosa Luxemburg was a revolutionary socialist and a member of the left-wing faction of the Social Democratic Party; in the women's section of the party she met Marie Stritt and they became life long friends.

They now had 14 nominations to be involved in the armistice negotiations: six statesman (Poincaré, Cambon, Lloyd George, Fischer, Bethmann-Hollweg, and Haase), five suffragettes (Pankhurst, Goldstein, Stritt, Zetkin and Rosa Luxemburg) and three distinguished scientists (Marie Curie, Albert Einstein and Max Weber). This seemed a good mixture of political experience and intelligent brains.

Samuel, Rory, Fritz, Wilhelm, Angus and Pierre now met to plan their next move. They decided that it was essential to keep all the troops along the front line aware of progress, so it was decided to use the recently invented telephone for this purpose. A carefully written bulletin would be produced each day and the operators were instructed to ensure that it passed precisely down the line to avoid any false rumours about the progress of negotiations. Next they communicated to military headquarters on both sides, and to all the governments who had troops involved, that they wanted the negotiations for an armistice to take place in Nancy and that they should be conducted, with the full support of their respective governments, by the fourteen listed above. There was predictable outrage from military headquarters.

Lloyd George fully supported this proposal to achieve peace without any further bloodshed and Fischer naturally supported the senior member of the British Empire in this proposal. Cambon prevailed long and hard on Poincaré, asking if he really wanted the responsibility for a generation of French women to be without husbands and a generation of French children to be without fathers? In the face of this argument, and the realisation that his two allies had governments which were amenable to an armistice, Poincaré finally relented. Haase adopted a similar tactic with Bethmann-Hollweg, who was less intransigent than Poincaré. The six immediately communicated to the fourteen nominees what had happened and urged them to agree to participate. Also the agreement was quickly communicated along the front line and then the six set out for Nancy to start arranging the negotiations. After inspecting the town it was decided that the Ducal Palace would be an appropriate location for the negotiations.

The six politicians were naturally pleased that they should be seen as those worthy of representing their country in such internationally important negotiations. The five suffragettes immediately agreed as they were delighted that it was recognised that women could provide an important contribution to such critical negotiations. Also, whilst they had all heard of each other, they had never all met together before and were much looking forward to this meeting. Marie Curie and Albert Einstein had great respect for each other and were pleased that it had been recognised that scientists could make a contribution in the political arena. As a sociologist Max Weber was fascinated to be able to work alongside a group of feminists who were certain to be making a big impact on society in the near future.

There was a mixed reaction abroad. The various pacifist groups in Europe and Australia were delighted, but there were militant xenophobic associations in all these countries, with people who considered such actions as cowardly and unpatriotic. Particularly outspoken were "the white feather brigade" in Britain and Australia; an obnoxious group of women who were themselves in no danger of fighting in the trenches. The gang of six realised that, if they were successful in achieving an armistice and cessation of hostilities, they were going to encounter a mixed reception when they returned home.

There was a fear that military headquarters, which had been sidelined, would do their utmost to interfere and frustrate the armistice, so both the German and Allied headquarters were advised that any attempt at interference by the military police would be met with overwhelming force, and that they risked their own troops standing aside and allowing troops from the opposing force to attack them. Naturally the senior generals were apoplectic at such a breach of military discipline, but they realised that they had no political support for a continuation of the war. Samuel pointed out that the 14 negotiators would need the support of experts to organise the aftermath if the negotiations were successful. Obviously the troop withdrawal would need to be carefully coordinated so that neither side could behave in an unscrupulous way and take advantage to launch an attack. He suggested that Colonel Monash would be an appropriate person to undertake this complicated and responsible task. It was obviously advantageous that Colonel Monash spoke very good German and could liaise effectively with both sides. Samuel also pointed out that it would be necessary to have an expert economist advise on the economic consequences of an armistice involving the demobilisation of soldiers and their return to civilian life. He had heard of a British economist who was highly regarded in both academic and administrative circles. His name was Maynard Keynes, so he recommended that he be invited to join the contingent in Nancy as an expert adviser.

Several weeks of preliminaries were required prior to the commencement of formal negotiations. It would take several weeks for Prime Minister Fisher and Vida Goldstein to travel from Australia. Also the various politicians would need to liaise with their governments about the position they should take and what concessions might be made. The French Council of Ministers supported Poincaré in insisting that there should be no concession on their demand that both Alsace and Lorraine be returned to them in full. As a former diplomat, this caused concern to Cambon who realised the consequences for negotiations of intransigence. In Germany Kaiser Wilhelm took advice from Hindenburg and Ludendorff and ignored Haase, whose Social Democratic party had won 35% of the vote in the recent Parliamentary election. Thus Germany arrived at the negotiations with an opening position as intransigent as the French. Lloyd George had consulted his Parliamentary colleagues and it had been agreed that he should take a pragmatic position and do his utmost to achieve a peaceful solution to this brutal conflict. When Fisher arrived from Australia he was enthusiastic in supporting Lloyd George's position and assured him that he would have an ally in the negotiations.

The five feminists were overjoyed at meeting each other and agreed that they should caucus together regularly to come up with an agreed position, and make it clear from the outset that they would not tolerate being disregarded and expected an equivalent time to speak as the men in the major plenary sessions. They agreed that Marie Curie should be invited to join them, as she was an inspiration to them all with regard to what women could achieve. When they heard from Marie Curie about the formation of this group, Albert Einstein and Max Weber asked if they might be able to attend at times as observers. They would be careful to stay in the background and not interfere in the women's deliberations; their position on the peace talks was obviously much closer to that of the women than that of the politicians. The feminists were obviously aware that male feminists did exist and they all admired John Stuart Mill and Henrik Ibsen, so they agreed that Albert Einstein and Max Weber could attend their group.

When Maynard Keynes arrived to perform his role as economic adviser, the feminists were also interested to meet him, as he was a member of the Bloomsbury group which included Virginia Woolf and Vanessa Bell. It occurred to them that the Nancy negotiations might lead not only to peace but also to the achievement of important feminist goals.

When they assembled for the first plenary session it was obvious that the six male politicians were quite daunted by the fact that they faced an equivalent collection of women. None of them had had to deal with a single female representative in their Parliament, so had little experience of male-female interaction outside their domestic life, where tradition had it at that the husband was dominant. After all, in the marriage ceremony the bride promised to obey her husband! The feminists had a lot of experience of public speaking and were very accomplished at it, so they made it clear that they expected to be treated with respect and as fully equal members of the armistice negotiations.

As his opening gambit Poincaré made it clear that he would not accept an armistice which did not include the full return to France of Alsace and Lorraine. Bethmann-Hollweg responded that the majority of Alsatians were ethnically German and spoke German so was it not logical that they be part of Germany? Goldstein and Zitkin, who were both involved in pacifist movements, responded to the French and German leaders: "This is a very bad start. The purpose of these negotiations is to come to a mutually agreeable peace treaty, so ultimately you two will have to moderate your positions. It was the machismo posturings of the military/political elite in France and Germany which led to this barbaric conflict. You both will have to place concern for your soldiers and their families before the pride of the xenophobes in your military and political commands. Women were not consulted about entry into this war but now we demand to be heard". Neither the French nor German leaders were accustomed to being spoken to in this way by anyone, let alone a couple of rebellious women. At this point Max Weber intervened and suggested that this might be a good point to adjourn for the day so that the participants might reflect on what had been said.

In the evening the six women, with Einstein and Weber, met to review the day's proceedings and plan future strategy. They had been watching the French and German leaders closely when Vida and Clara made their opening statement. They had noted expressions of both fury and concern on the faces of the two leaders. There were four journalists accredited to the peace talks so that the public in the four countries could be apprised of the proceedings. One in particular, an Australian woman called Louise Mack, who had been reporting from the front line for two English papers, the Daily Mail and the Evening News, was sure to give an accurate account of anything the feminists contributed to the proceedings. She had been sending back graphic accounts of the harsh realities of trench warfare and the current impasse, which she predicted to be prolonged. Given what Vida and Clara had said regarding the lack of consultation with women about the declaration of hostilities, and the need to consider family welfare, both leaders recognised that they would be cast in a very bad light and incur a considerable amount of opprobrium if they did not make a serious attempt to achieve a compromise. In the face of this ultimatum from the women Poincaré and Bethmann-Hollweg set off for Berlin and Paris with Cambon and Haas to consult with their Parliaments and chief military advisers. The remaining ten participants and the four news reporters took advantage of this interlude to explore the art nouveau delights of Nancy, which included, naturally, Brasserie Excelsior where they consumed some delicious seafood.

When they reconvened, it was suggested by Max Weber that they should be addressed by Maynard Keynes on the economic consequences of a prolonged war of attrition. The human and social costs of such an event were obvious, but it was also important for these negotiations that the participants were also aware of the economic implications. Maynard began by explaining that his name was pronounced Canes and saying how pleased he was at meeting the feminists, whom he had heard about from his friend Virginia Woolf, and she had asked him to pass on her regards and best wishes for the peace talks. He began with some history of warfare. Throughout history there had been many prolonged conflicts but they had tended to be between standing armies and had not involved mass conscription. The 1870 conflict between France and Germany had involved conscription and mass armies, but it had only lasted six months. This war was only in its fourth month but it was clear, particularly from what had happened at Ypres, that it was developing into a long war of attrition, and some military experts he had consulted were pessimistic that it could last several years at the cost of hundreds of thousands of lives. If so, there were serious economic implications of such prolonged warfare involving mass armies of men. These men had been diverted from productive activities in the fields and the factories. In many cases women had been drafted in as substitute labour, but often it was in the manufacture of munitions, rather than in replacing the peacetime production of men. The loss of agricultural production in Britain could largely be dealt with by imports from America, but the superiority of British naval forces meant that Germany was likely to incur shortages of both food and some raw materials for industrial production. The loss of manufacturing capacity meant that all countries' capital stock would run down during the war; the housing stock would deteriorate as the necessary maintenance was not being performed; likewise the railway networks would fall into disrepair if they were not regularly maintained. In the case of Britain, in particular, which was a leading world producer and exporter of manufactured goods, there would be a serious shock to the balance of payments. In Germany he foresaw a particular danger for agriculture as the supply of nitrates were diverted from fertiliser production to the explosives industry. The French agricultural capacity would be diminished by the damage this war was doing to the land. Britain was certain to end up being severely indebted to the USA.

Keynes said that he could go on, but it must already be apparent that a continuation of this war would have serious economic consequences for all countries involved. He ended by saying that it was unusual for a major war to have positive consequences, but he sincerely hoped that the current acceptance of women in the workforce would be permanent, and that hereafter women would be treated with equality throughout society with equal access to education and employment. The feminists were already impressed with Keynes because of his position as a conscientious objector, and now there was a burst of applause for his forthright statement demanding economic equality for women. Some of the male politicians looked aghast.

When the formal plenary session resumed Poincaré and Bethmann-Hollweg explained that they had reported full details of the proceedings to their respective Parliaments and had emphasised that they accepted that there now needed to be some form of compromise. Lloyd George responded that he and Fischer were pleased to hear this, as they had all along been in support of compromise. Cambon and Haase reported that the military command on both sides had maintained their belligerent, xenophobic positions, but had been unnerved when it was suggested that they might go and spend a month in a trench on the front line. The feminists and the scientists welcomed this progress and suggested that it was now time to get down to the nitty-gritty of the armistice details. Perhaps they could split into subgroups initially, with the four German and French statesmen meeting together to see if they could move towards some common ground. The feminists and scientists meanwhile would do some brainstorming in the hope of coming up with some innovative solution. It was decided to take a couple of days over this before they all met together in the next plenary session.

Bethmann-Hollweg suggested that perhaps Lorraine could be returned to France on condition that they continue to meet German iron ore requirements in full at a 10% discount off the prevailing world price. Poincaré suggested that, in view of the past history of Alsace, and its ethnically diverse population, it was worth considering whether it might be established as a small independent state like Luxembourg. They consulted Lloyd George and Fischer, who confirmed that they agreed that these seemed sensible compromises to avoid the human, social and economic costs of this war. Especially as it was now apparent that it would drag on for years.

The feminists, who naturally were enamoured of voting, suggested that the people of the two provinces be asked to choose for themselves which country they should be incorporated into. The electorate should consist of everyone over the age of 21.

Max Weber said that he had been reading some articles written by a young Frenchman called Jean Monnet. He was suggesting a quasi-federal arrangement under which there would be common management of the French and Rhineland coal and steel industry. Each country would concede sovereignty to a supranational body which would be mandated to pursue policies in their mutual interest. As an example he pointed to the Federation of Australia in 1901, in which the six colonies, had agreed to concede certain powers to a new Commonwealth government. This had been achieved by a vote across the six colonies. The two physicists where impressed by Monnet's suggestion as a fresh and innovative approach to an old problem.

They next met in plenary session to review the various proposals in the hope of coming to a mutually acceptable conclusion. After a lengthy discussion of the various proposals they ended up agreeing to a combination of what the feminists and Max Weber had suggested. The historical conflict between France and Germany had been generated by statesman and military commanders, and in this day and age it did seem appropriate for the population at large to be consulted. It was obvious that the Alsace population should be consulted about whether they were to be French, German or independent, as Luxembourg was. It also made sense that the two countries should stop squabbling over the iron and coal resources of Lorraine and the Rhineland, and instead participate in this cooperative, supra-national arrangement. In the future it is possible that it could become more widespread across Europe, as federation had been successful in the three "New World" countries: America, Australia and Canada. Bethmann Hollweg and Poincaré now set off to take these suggestions back to their respective governments. They were accompanied respectively by Haase and Cambon.

Before Poincaré left for Paris, Lloyd George and Fischer met with him and indicated that if the French were in anyway an impediment to these peace suggestions they would withdraw their troops and leave the French to fight alone. Naturally this threat concentrated Poincaré's mind. There had been some food riots in Berlin and Kaiser Wilhelm was becoming concerned that they could escalate if this war dragged on, as was becoming increasingly apparent. In particular there was this wretched woman called Rosa Luxembourg, who had been organising an anti-conscription campaign and liaising with the French socialist Jean Jaurès to organise a general strike of French and German workers in the event of war breaking out. The fact that Luxembourg and Zetkin were members of this peace negotiating group in Nancy added to his insecurity. His cousin Tsar Nicholas had been facing revolutionary activity for most of the century, so Kaiser Wilhelm was nervous that it might spread to Germany. This meant that the political leadership in both Berlin and Paris were under considerable pressure, so, despite much huffing and puffing from the senior military, both the French and German governments accepted the peace terms and the four political representatives scurried off to Nancy with the good news.

Naturally the fourteen were delighted with this news and decided that they should set off to Brassiere Excelsior for a celebration to which they invited Maynard Keynes and Louise Mack, who had already filed a report with her British and Australian newspapers. Next day the fourteen assembled in plenary section along with Keynes and Monash. Monash was needed to explain how the troop withdrawal on both sides would be organised and supervised. Keynes was needed to explain how this quasi-federal arrangement would be constructed and implemented. The first thing they decided was that the troops on the front line should be advised that peace terms had been agreed by France and Germany and all that remained now was to work out the precise terms of the agreement and have it implemented. In the interim, strict terms of the truce should be respected by both sides. The second thing they decided was that the six troops, who had instigated this process, should be invited to Nancy, so that they could join with them in another celebration at Brasserie Excelsior.

Back where it all began, Rory and Fritz ran up white flags and the Australians British and Germans charged out to embrace each other. It was suggested that they all go back to the café in a nearby village where Fergus had been buying their supply of plonk. The British were somewhat surprised at the enthusiasm by which Fergus was welcomed by the Madame. She and her French patrons were alarmed at the presence of the German troops, but Angus quickly intervened to explain that a peace treaty has just been agreed, so the war was over. He also explained that these German troops had not been responsible for the war and had been found, during the impromptu Christmas truce, to be very fine fellows. Madame noted that Fergus was in full agreement, so she shouted "Vive la Paix" and ordered drinks on the house.

The Germans had noticed a soccer pitch in the village so it was suggested that the Richmond team should try their hand at the game, consequently it was arranged that there would be a German versus Richmond soccer match the next day. It was explained to the local French population that the Australians played a game in which you could handle the ball, kick it high and bump your opponent vigorously. The word got around so the local population turned up in force to watch a game between their traditional opponents Germany and a strange group of men from far away who were accustomed to bumping their opponents and picking up the ball to kick it long distances. The one thing which they would obviously be very good at was the position of Goalie. The Richmond backman Bob Fraser was the obvious candidate to play in goal and Peter Wood would obviously be a winger. Naturally Rory's place was as centre forward but he didn't know how he would cope without being able to touch the ball.

When the local French referee began the match he did emphasise to the Australians that they could try to win the ball by kicking it from underneath the feet of the Germans but they couldn't bump them. He also had to explain the offside rule which was a mystery to the Australians and quite hard to understand. Peter Wood was much faster than his opponent but he couldn't keep the ball with him as he ran, in the way his opponent could, so he kicked the ball well ahead and sprinted after it. Often this proved effective but just as often a German defender pounced on it. Just occasionally Peter's tactic was effective and he managed to pass the ball to Rory. Rory was able to kick the ball very hard and a couple of times he did evade the goalkeeper, so Richmond ended up with a respectable score of two. Naturally Germany dominated possession of the ball and they peppered the goal with shots, but Bob Fraser was vigorously jumping around and clearing most of the shots on goal; nevertheless the Germans came out the winners with five goals.

A scout from the local Amiens football club had come to watch this strange game and he was particularly impressed with Bob Fraser's performance as goalkeeper and the speed of Peter Wood. He knew that Olympique Lillois would be very interested to recruit them, and he believed that it would not take too long to teach Peter Wood how to dribble the ball as he ran. Bob and Peter were both married and each had a small child; also they were very happy with their place in the Richmond team so they declined his kind offer.

After the game they had the luxury of their first shower in months. Next they intended to set off for the local café again and this time to eat some real French food to accompany the wine. Some said that they had deduced the relationship between Fergus and Madame, so they thought they would try their luck with the local mademoiselles. Rory reminded them that some had wives, fiancées or long-term girlfriends so they should consider themselves off-limits. Only those completely unattached were at liberty to try and charm these local ladies, and that might be difficult if none of the mademoiselles spoke English, as he was not aware that any of his team spoke French. To Rory's surprise, Louis Strong, the other Richmond wingman, disclosed that his widowed mother was French and therefore he spoke perfect French, and that they might have deduced his parenthood from his first name. As he was unattached, and quite familiar with the French way of life, he felt at liberty and optimistic in dealing with the local mademoiselles, and he knew that his mother would be delighted. Australians were not noted for their bilingual skills, so his teammates were startled at having such an erudite member of the squad.

They were even more impressed when they got to the café and saw Louis immediately launch into a discussion with a group of French women. They had seen him sprinting around like Peter and asked how he had acquired such a knowledge of French when he lived 12,000 miles away. When he explained that his mother was French they were interested to know in what part of France she had been born and how she had come to live in Australia. He explained that she had actually been born in the East End of London amongst the Huguenot Community, which had fled France because of persecution for their religious beliefs. The mademoiselles knew their French history and quickly proceeded to apologise for the behaviour of their ancestors. Louis explained that where he lived in an inner Melbourne suburb there was considerable animosity between Irish Catholics and Protestants so he was familiar with religious bigotry, although fortunately violence did not extend beyond schoolboy scuffles between the catholic and state schools. He was particularly successful in charming Claudette who explained that she lived with her sister, as her mother had died in childbirth and her father was away fighting at the front. She suggested that he might find it a relief to sleep in a bed for a change after all those dangerous and uncomfortable months in the trenches. Because her parents were absent it meant that there was a vacant grand lit in her house which he would be welcome to sleep in. Louis realised from his quasi-French upbringing that it would be most unchivalrous to refuse such an invitation, so he clutched her hand, bad farewell to his teammates and sped off with Claudette to explore the pleasures of a French grand lit.

Next morning Louise Mack arrived to invite the band of six to come to Nancy to spend an evening with the peace negotiating team to celebrate their success. When Samuel, Rory, Angus, Wilhelm, Fritz and Pierre arrived in Nancy they were taken by Louise on a tour of its art nouveau delights, including Brasserie Excelsior, where they were to eat that evening. Richmond was an inner industrial suburb of Melbourne with lots of factories and tiny timber houses so Rory was overwhelmed by the elegance and beauty of Nancy. As it was the capital of Lorraine he resolved that this is where he and his fiancée should spend their honeymoon. Louise wanted to talk with Samuel and Rory in particular as she was fascinated at how a couple of young Australian men had come to be instrumental in achieving peace in Europe. She learnt that Samuel Harcourt was the son of a Jewish family which had emigrated to Australia after the Odessa pogrom of 1821. His family kept to strict Jewish traditions and after he had finished his history studies he was expected to switch to law and become a barrister. In contrast, Rory's background was Irish, dating back first to the convict period and later to those fleeing the Irish famine. He lived with his parents and five siblings in one of those tiny timber houses in Richmond. His father was a truck driver so it was difficult for his mother to feed a family of six children, which meant that they all had to seek employment once they were fourteen. Rory had been lucky to be born with superior athletic skills, which enabled him to be a star Australian footballer. The club had arranged for him to be apprenticed to a master plumber who was a fanatical Richmond supporter. He was more than happy to pay Rory above the normal rate and allow him time off for his football training. Nevertheless Rory and Lorraine were not planning on an ostentatious wedding ceremony. Louise had now an excellent article for her Australian paper, about how a young Jewish student and a working-class footballer, both from Melbourne, had laid the foundation for peace in Europe.

When they next assembled in a plenary session, Colonel Monash was invited to address them on how the troop withdrawal and demilitarisation was to be organised. He said that it was obvious that troops and artillery should withdraw behind the front line in a coordinated fashion and at an equivalent number of miles each day. A contingent of Spanish and Scandinavian military should act as peacekeepers to ensure that there was strict adherence to these conditions. After the Allied and German forces had pulled back significantly behind their borders the process of destroying artillery and machine guns could begin. There would have to be negotiations about how much of this armament could be retained for purely defensive purposes, but it would have to be minimal. It would have to be accompanied by regular and thorough inspections of French and German industry to ensure that there was no clandestine production of any form of military equipment. Also much of the senior military would have to be stood down and in particular this had to include Joffre, Moltke and Haig. Finally he suggested that there should be some form of acknowledgment for the band of six. This could not be a military medal as their achievement had not been incurred on the field of battle. All countries had a system of civilian honours so he recommended that the four countries involved should give careful thought to what was appropriate for their member or members of this band of six. As an afterthought he suggested that Louise Mack should also be recommended for a civilian honour, as her brilliant reports from the front had brought to the attention of the general public how horrible and futile this trench war was. After fielding some questions from the fourteen, he set off for Madrid and Copenhagen to secure Spanish and Scandinavian agreement to act as peacekeepers.

Next they settled down to discuss how the terms of the agreement were to be implemented. Emmeline Pankhurst said that each region should choose, in a preferential system, which State they wished to be part of. The electorate should consist of all adults. The Alsatians were to be asked whether they wanted to be French, German or independent. These three options would have to be listed in order of preference and, if there was not a clear majority for the one which topped the poll, then second preferences of the one which came third would be redistributed amongst the other two. The Lorrains would be asked whether they wished to be French or German. They would also be asked, along with the Rhineland Germans, whether they would cede control of their mutual iron and coal resources to a supra-national authority. Keynes suggested that this authority could be located in Strasbourg and that its governing membership should be elected by the residents of the two resource-rich areas. Its powers would be limited to the extraction of coal and iron ore; the production and distribution of steel. It would have an equal number of French and German representatives, with a leadership which rotated on an annual basis. The fourteen negotiators agreed in general with what Monash and Pankhurst had suggested but Poincaré and Bethmann-Hollweg expressed some concern about sacking Joffre and Moltke. On the other hand Lloyd George said he would be delighted to sack Haig. The French and German statesmen were told that the whole purpose of this exercise was to achieve an enduring peace and consequently they had to reorganise their military as a less belligerent body. Cambon and Haase pointed out that Louise Mack's articles for the English papers had been translated into French and German, and circulated widely in those countries. The general population therefore would be aware of the ineptitude of the military leaders and have no sympathy for their departure. The four statesman then returned to Berlin and Paris to explain what had been agreed about the voting arrangements for the two territories and the proposed iron and steel community. They also explained the procedures for armament destruction and the inspection regime to ensure there was no illicit production of armaments in the future. Finally they enforced the retirement of Joffre and Moltke.

Nancy's Town Clerk and his senior staff were tasked with arranging the voting procedures required by the peace treaty. Meanwhile Monash had been successful in obtaining the cooperation of the Spanish and Scandinavian governments in providing troops to oversee a coordinated withdrawal from the front line, and to begin the immediate destruction of artillery pieces and machine guns.

Chapter Three

Reaction to Peace Terms

UNDERSTANDABLY this varied between the two countries whose land was in dispute, and the two countries which had come to the aid of the French. The right wing tabloids in both France and Germany were furious and depicted the four statesmen who were involved in the peace negotiations as traitors. In France Le Petit Journal thundered about not having reclaimed outright Lorraine and Alsace, "which was traditional French territory." It demanded the immediate resignation of Poincaré and the reinstatement immediately of Joffre. It was also contemptuous of any supra-national arrangement with the detested Germans. Le Temps, predictably, took a more thoughtful and balanced view. It published a long article setting out details of the long running conflict there had been with the Prussians/Germans. It stressed the futility of this conflict and the desirability of achieving an enduring peace. One necessary ingredient of this was to have a far less belligerent military. A promising ingredient was the suggested supra-national arrangements for iron and steel extraction and steel production. This could possibly be extended to other areas and bring the two nations together in harmony, rather than in conflict. There was a similar dichotomy amongst the German press. Berliner Post was furious that, under the peace terms, they risked losing Lorraine and/or Alsace, two territories with significant populations of German speakers, for which they had fought long and hard. Also they considered it bizarre that there was any suggestion that they should join together with France in any type of supra-national authority. They called for Bethmann-Hollweg to go immediately and be replaced by Moltke. The Suddeutsche Zeitung accepted that the human and economic costs of what inevitably appeared to be a protracted war could not be defended when there was a reasonable chance that Lorraine and Alsace would remain German via the ballot box. After years of conflict it was time to make peace with the French, and the proposed iron and steel Federation could be an important precursor of that.

In Britain there was also a divergence of view amongst the press but it was not quite as vitriolic. Predictably, the Daily Telegraph and the Daily Mail were outraged by the participation of Emmeline Pankhurst and Colonel Monash in this peace process; their misogyny and anti-Semitism being readily apparent. They were incensed by the sacking of Haig and demanded that he be immediately reinstated. In contrast, the Manchester Guardian, which had vigorously campaigned against entry into this war, was delighted that peace had broken out. In particular they were overjoyed that Emmeline Pankhurst had been not just one of the fourteen peace negotiators but had been responsible for arranging the voting procedures for the two provinces and the populations of the two areas in the proposed iron and steel community. It was obvious that the enfranchisement of all British adults could be no longer delayed.

In Australia the news coverage was dominated by the role which Samuel and Rory had played in the peace process, as Louise Mack's articles had made their efforts widely known to the general public. It was seen as very confusing because there had been such great enthusiasm when the war had begun, and now it was being brought to a peaceful end in a process initiated by a couple of local lads. There were some mutterings of cowardice, but not around Richmond where Rory was the local hero. The Women's Peace Army, which had been founded by Vida Goldstein, made sure that the public was aware of her involvement as a member of the peace negotiating team. The Melbourne Jewish community was delighted at the prominent role which Samuel Harcourt and Colonel Monash had played in the achievement of peace.

Louise Mack had discovered in her interview with Rory that he had a fiancée in Richmond, whom he had been intending to marry earlier in the year. Louise decided that it would make an interesting article for the Women's Page of the Melbourne Age if she could get an interview with Rory's fiancée. She had her address, as Rory had bought a Cross of Lorraine when he had been in Nancy and asked Louise to deliver it when she returned to Melbourne. So one evening Louise knocked on the front door of a timber cottage in Richmond to be met by a small pretty woman. This was quite a surprise as Rory was at least 6 foot tall, so there must be at least a foot difference between the two. Lorraine explained that this was not a problem, but she did have to stand on tiptoes to kiss Rory. When Louise produced Rory's present, Lorraine was puzzled because they were both Protestants and not accustomed to wearing crosses round their neck. Louise quickly explained that it was a Cross of Lorraine, so Rory had decided that she should have one to wear. Lorraine was delighted to hear this and explained that, although Rory had the reputation of being a hard man as a footballer, in private he was very romantic so this was typical of him. Louise learned that Lorraine was a ladies hairdresser and worked at an exclusive salon in the suburb of Toorak. It was not far from Richmond and just involved two short tram journeys, but socially and economically it was poles apart. Toorak was where the richest people in Melbourne lived in Grand Estates with very large houses. One even had wallabies roaming in its large garden. This inevitably meant that Lorraine had to be a very talented hairdresser, because she was dressing the hair of women who were imitating those who frequented the large houses of Belgravia.

Lorraine explained that she had been engaged to Rory for quite some time and therefore she had been very upset that their wedding had been deferred. Rory had written and explained that he had deduced the fun which Louis and Claudette must have been having and also Fergus and Madame. Therefore he wanted her to put together their savings and try and find a cheap passage to Southampton. He was expecting to make some money from newspaper interviews in Britain and France and perhaps even in Germany. He was sure that they would be allowed to marry in Saint Martin's in the Fields, which was a famous church in Trafalgar Square. He planned to take her to Nancy for their honeymoon as it was the capital city of Lorraine. Louise produced some postcards of Nancy, which Rory had bought for Lorraine and she was staggered by the beauty of the place. Louise got some background information on Lorraine's family and schooling; also on how she had met Rory and what their plans were for the future and then scurried off to write her article.

The Age was delighted with the article and paid her handsomely, which she intended to split evenly with Lorraine. Everyone in "Toorak Ladies Haut Coiffure" was thrilled with the article in The Age, but sad that they might soon be losing their brightest star. Lorraine's clients were aware that she was engaged to Rory Hart and often wanted to chat about how they met and what he was like as a boyfriend. Most were obviously quite jealous, especially those who had seen him play in those very brief shorts. Now that they had read Louise's article, they were even more impressed, both by his role in ending this dreadful war, in which some of their brothers and sons were involved, and also by his clearly romantic nature. Lady Bailey, who was the doyenne of the Toorak social set and had a son with the rank of captain on the front line in France, invited all of Lorraine's clients to tea the following Thursday afternoon. When they were all assembled and enjoying some of Paterson's famous cakes she explained the purpose of the gathering. Lorraine had been attending to their hair with great skill and cheerfulness for several years and she had a fiancé who had been instrumental in bringing an end to this dreadful war, and had perhaps saved some of their sons or brothers from a horrible death. Therefore she recommended that they all contribute generously to a fund which would ensure that Lorraine had a comfortable passage to England and that the couple could have a splendid wedding and honeymoon. Naturally everyone present agreed that this was a commendable idea and they were all generous in their contributions.

A couple of the exclusive Collins Street dress shops had also been impressed by the article in The Age and offered to provide Lorraine with a wedding gown and a trousseau, which included shoes to fit her tiny feet. They hoped that Lorraine would be photographed coming out of Saint Martin's in the Fields so that they could display it in their window. The famous Melbourne men's outfitter, Henry Bucks, made a comparable offer for Rory, whose measurements they obtained from Richmond Football Club, so Lorraine was going to end up with more than one trunk of luggage to take with her on board.

When Louis Strong's mother read in The Age that Lorraine was to spend her honeymoon in Nancy she was much impressed and called around to see Lorraine and offered to teach her some French. She explained that they would have much more fun exploring Nancy if one of them could speak French. Richmond state school had no provision for foreign language tuition, so Lorraine had never been exposed to the idea of being bilingual, but she had excelled at the English language so she was prepared to try out French. Simone Strong had some basic French grammar books which she had used years ago when she taught Louis how to speak French. Lorraine knew from Rory's letters that Louis' command of French must be considerable given his success in wooing Claudette. She borrowed Simone's books and arranged to visit her every other night for a lesson.

When Lorraine arrived at the salon, Lady Bailey was there with a cheque for a larger amount of money than Lorraine had ever possessed in her life. She was staggered by the generosity and asked Lady Bailey for names of all the contributors so that she could write to each one personally.

There was an Orient Line ship leaving for Southampton in two weeks and Lorraine now decided that she could afford a standard second-class cabin rather than the cheap one she had been contemplating. She also decided that she could afford to buy a camera, so that she could send back photos of her wedding and of Nancy to her mother and all the other people who had been so generous to her. Lorraine's cabin was crowded for a send off: all her family, and her colleagues from Toorak Ladies' Haut Coiffure, were there, plus all the wives and fiancées of the Richmond footballers. In addition some of her neighbours had come along as this was their first opportunity to be on a big ocean liner. When the announcement came for all non-passengers to leave the ship, Lorraine got lots of tearful hugs and best wishes for her forthcoming marriage.

As the big liner slowly pulled out into Port Phillip Bay Lorraine set about unpacking her trunk and setting up her cabin. Simone had lent her a French grammar book, a simple story book for beginners and a dictionary, which she placed on her bedside table along with a photo of Rory. She was so excited that she couldn't sleep, so she got out her French story book to expand her vocabulary and try thinking in French. Next morning the Purser approached the Captain, as he was eating his breakfast in the dining room, to tell him that Lorraine was currently enjoying her breakfast in the second-class dining room. "Do we have a vacant first-class cabin?" was his reply. When the Purser confirmed that there were several, the captain instructed that Lorraine be given the best available with his compliments and that she should be invited to join him at dinner this evening. The little girl from Richmond was starting to be overwhelmed by the notoriety she had acquired because of her forthcoming marriage to Rory. She readily accepted the invitation and a steward helped her to move her belongings to a first-class cabin, which was quite spacious and had a beautiful view of the ocean.

She spent some of the day studying French and the rest of it exploring the first class facilities, and enjoyed watching the passengers playing various deck sports. Her trousseau, so generously provided by the haute couture shops of Collins Street, contained some elegant evening dresses so she laid one out for her dinner invitation. She might be small, but she was very pretty and quite stunning in her elegant evening dress, so all eyes turned as she entered the dining room at 8 o'clock. The Captain stood up to greet her and motioned her to sit beside him. He explained to his other guests at the Captain's table who she was, whom she was to marry and why he was honoured to have her at his side. Her fellow guests were interested to know all about her and how it felt to be the fiancée of a very brilliant footballer, who now was also a famous peacemaker. When she informed them that they were spending their honeymoon in Nancy two couples at the other end of the table became quite excited. They had been in Victoria exploring suitable territory for wine-growing. They were vintners from the famous French wine region of Burgundy, which was just south of Nancy, so they would be honoured if the young couple came to visit them when their time in Nancy was over. When Lorraine explained that she was in the process of learning French, the two wives offered their assistance, so it was organised what one would come for an hour in the morning to help with grammar and engage in conversation whilst the other would come in the afternoon for an hour's conversation.

Each morning after her French studies, Lorraine went out to stroll on the deck and, as by now all the first class passengers knew who she was, many wanted to chat to her. There was an elderly English Countess who told to her that she lived in Belgravia. In view of what she had heard from the Toorak ladies, this was of great interest to Lorraine. The Countess explained that her son, who was a Major in the

Coldstream Guards, was away fighting at the front and she had been panic-stricken because he was her only son and therefore the only person available to inherit the Earldom. She had noted that Lorraine was very elegantly dressed in evening gowns with shoes to match, but the one thing she lacked was a nice necklace. She enquired if Lorraine would object to her buying an appropriate necklace in the ship's shop as a thank you for Rory's involvement in bringing this horrible war to a peaceful conclusion, so that she could have her son safely back in England. Also she would like to invite the two of them for dinner in Belgravia when they got back from their European honeymoon. Lorraine was becoming accustomed to the generosity of others and graciously accepted this generous offer from the Countess. So Lorraine spent her days learning and practising French, playing deck quoits with the other passengers and dining in style with the Captain and his guests. Because there were two Burgundy vintners on board she also acquired a lot of knowledge of French wine. They explained the fragrant nature of the Pinot Noir grape and the crisp steely finish of the Chardonnay grape: the two grapes which defined Burgundy. In the evenings she joined in the dancing and it was obvious that a couple of the young men would have tried their luck with her if she hadn't been the fiancée of Rory Hunter.

When the liner entered the English Channel she became particularly excited and made sure everything was packed ready for a swift departure. She had bade farewell to the Countess and the French vintners and wives. She had all their addresses safely written down and promised to contact them after her honeymoon. To greet Rory she put on a tight fitting jumper, which she knew he would approve of, and a straight skirt which was daringly knee length. Rory was very strong and when he embraced her she almost felt she might faint. They kissed and cuddled all the way to Waterloo station where the whole Richmond team was there to welcome them. They all wanted to kiss her and when it came to Louis' turn she spoke to him in French and explained that his mother had commenced her tuition and then it had continued on board the ship with the two Burgundian ladies. He was mightily impressed with her fluency and offered to engage in conversation practice whenever she had time. Rory was startled and asked what was going on, so she explained how helpful and generous Simone had been, and how her French was now going to make it much easier and more fun when they were in Nancy. She now got another of his bone crunching hugs, and he said that he now knew that she was not just very pretty but also very clever. He had noted how smartly she was dressed and enquired how expensive that had been. When she explained that his fame as a peacemaker meant that she had been given a substantial sum from the Toorak ladies, and a wedding dress and trousseau from the Haute Couture shops in Collins Street he was staggered. More so when she told him that he also had a trousseau from Henry Bucks. As a Richmond boy he had never felt easy about entering that shop, but now he owned a whole outfit of Henry Bucks' stylish clothes.

He immediately enquired if the Australian public knew that Samuel Harcourt had played an equal, if not more significant, role in the process than he had. In particular Samuel's lessons to both the British and Germans had served to concentrate the minds of the troops, who previously had not known the various past alliances in conflict of the European powers. In particular Samuel had explained to them the complicated set of alliances which had led up to this war. Lorraine explained that the interview which Louise Mack had conducted with them both in Nancy had been published in full detail in the Australian papers. Therefore everyone would be aware of their joint achievement, and she knew that the Australian Jewish community was delighted that Louise had disclosed the role played by Samuel and Colonel Monash in the peace process.

Rory was relieved to hear this and explained that they were now off to stay at the Ritz; in two single rooms for the next two nights, but on Saturday, after the wedding, they were to have the honeymoon suite. The Ritz had kindly offered them free accommodation and meals until they left for their honeymoon in Nancy. They had rooms overlooking Green Park and after having a luxurious bath Lorraine dressed in one of her elegant evening dresses and put on the necklace which the Countess had so generously given her. After showering, Rory proceeded to dress from head to toe in his new Henry Bucks outfit. Louis had brought Claudette with him to London and, as the only other couple amongst the Richmond team, they were to join Rory and Lorraine for dinner. Inevitably the sommelier handed the wine list to Rory and was startled when he handed it to Lorraine and said "you should order the plonk". Lorraine could not restrain herself from giggling and said to Louis, in French, "Why didn't you explain it to them?"

"Oh I thought it was rather fun and I didn't want to appear a know-all," Louis replied in English.

"What's going on?" said Rory.

"The French put the adjective after the noun not before as we do. What you were wanting was vin blanc, in other words white wine, but technically you were just saying white."

Claudette now joined in the giggling and told them that Madame had quickly recognised what was going on and told Louis not to spoil the fun. Rory now started laughing and said to Lorraine that nevertheless he still thought she was the knowledgeable one to order the plonk.

The Ritz wine list was many pages long but Lorraine turned to the burgundy section and particularly to Chablis and Volnay. She chose a premier cru from the estate of one of her new friends and another premier cru from Volnay. When the sommelier returned to take the order from a young woman from the colonies he was very surprised at the sophistication of her order. They started on the Chablis and Rory was startled by how smooth and delicious it was compared with the plonk he had been drinking for months. Lorraine explained that there are very many wine regions in France and that Burgundy and Bordeaux were the most revered for producing the finest quality wine, but there were many other areas that produced wine of an inferior quality. What he was accustomed to drinking was vin ordinaire. Rory next informed them that he had consulted his Richmond teammates and that they understood that, in the circumstances, he should ask Samuel to be his best man. All Lorraine's friends were back in Melbourne, so she asked Claudette if she would be her bridesmaid. Liberty in Regent Street had offered to provide a dress for a bridesmaid, so next morning Lorraine and Claudette set off for Regent Street and Lorraine took the opportunity to ask if Claudette had any advice about being a good lover.

Meanwhile Samuel was taking the opportunity of doing all things Jewish in London. First he set off for the famous Jewish restaurant, Blooms, in Aldgate to order salt beef and latkas. Later he contacted some Jewish relatives of his mother, and they invited him to their home in Golders

Green for a Friday evening dinner. So that there would be a young person of his own age to be appropriate company, they invited a young neighbour called Golda. She was pretty and vivacious and keen to know how he had come to be instrumental in ending the horrible war and what life was like for Jews in Australia. She offered to take him to the East End of London to show him where Jews had first settled when they had fled here and she invited him to her home for dinner next Friday evening so he could meet her parents. Naturally they enquired about his parents and the Jewish community in Melbourne. They were pleased to hear that he intended to train to be a barrister, but they were surprised to hear that he was a keen footballer and played this game they had read about in Louise Mack's report of the initial stages of the peace process. Golda and Samuel's relationship soon moved from affection to passion, so he proposed to her, but explained that he did have to return to Melbourne to complete his studies so how would that affect her decision? She replied that she wanted desperately to accept but she would have to consult her parents about her moving to the other side of the world. Naturally they said that they would be very sad to lose her, but they realised that Samuel would be a fine husband with excellent prospects. They also knew that there was a significant Jewish community in Melbourne, which was very happy with their lives there. So the young couple were engaged immediately and Golda's mother set about arranging a marriage in the Golders Green synagogue.

Chapter Four

Progress on Peace

COLONEL Monash arranged for the Spanish and Scandinavian troops to muster in Nancy. He explained the delicate nature of the task and that they should try desperately not to antagonise the French or German troops. A mixed contingent of Spanish and Scandinavian troops would be deployed on each side of the front. This was to ensure that there could be no allegation that one country's troops were more or less harsh than the other. He would supervise their progress and alternate on a daily basis between the two sides. After each side had withdrawn 10 miles from the front line, they would begin the process of armament destruction. This would be coordinated so that an equivalent amount of ordinance from each country would be destroyed on a daily basis. He had noted that both countries had deployed armies with a much higher than normal contingent of officers. This clearly was to ensure maximum diplomacy in this delicate operation. Monash approved of this and said that the four armies involved should respect the chain of military command, and that he would inform senior officers in the French and German armies that this was to be so. He certainly could not have a Spanish lieutenant ordering a German colonel about!

Meanwhile the Nancy Town Clerk was making steady progress with the voting arrangements. The elections were to take place on a Saturday and polling stations would be set up in all local schools, but establishing the electoral register was a nightmare. The names of most eligible men could be taken from the records of those liable to pay local taxes, which in most cases was the male "head of the household". But there was no equivalent record of women, nor of young men who had yet to marry and form a household. He consulted Emmeline Pankhurst and explained the problem. She went off to consult her fellow feminists to consider a solution. They were quite familiar with this phenomenon of women being written out of history and existence. They suggested that it should be widely publicised that all adult women were eligible to vote and encouraged to do so. At each polling station a local Mayor or Alderman should be present with his wife to identify the eligible local women. If any woman was denied a vote she would be able to appeal to an assembly of the wives of all local male taxpayers. The Town Clerk thought that this was an excellent solution to a difficult problem and asked Emmeline Pankhurst to pass on his gratitude to the group of feminists. In Lorraine there would be two groups of protagonists and in Alsace there would be three. They were to be equivalently funded and to be given equal space in all local newspapers. Any evidence of voter intimidation would be properly investigated and guilty culprits would face a prison sentence.

There were hustings in all the villages, which were well attended and produced robust debate. Some of the husbands took it upon themselves to instruct their wives how they should vote, but the women knew that they would be voting in secret so just listened attentively to keep the peace, whist determining that they would express their own preference in the ballot box.

Local school teachers had been recruited to conduct the elections; they had copies of the local tax registers and at each polling station they had the local Alderman and his wife to confirm eligible female voters. At the finish of polling, it was these local teachers who counted the votes. The peace negotiators had been hoping that there would be a clear victory for one side or the other. They feared that a close vote could ultimately lead to a re-emergence of conflict in the future.

In Lorraine the results were clear cut: 62% opted to be part of France and 38% to be part of Germany. It was not so in Alsace where 45% voted to be German, 30% to be French and 25% to be independent. When the independent votes were re-distributed it was 59% for Germany and 41% for France. Before the voting had taken place it had been made clear by the public authorities that there should be no exuberant celebrations by the victors, and that these communities should be magnanimous in victory. The French government was delighted that it had regained Lorraine with its beautiful capital Nancy. They grudgingly accepted the loss of Alsace, whose political status had been disputed for centuries. The German government was delighted that, after centuries of dispute, Alsace was now to be part of Germany. The loss of Lorraine was partially compensated for by the new arrangement for an iron and steel community, which meant that they would retain access to iron reserves within the new cooperative arrangement. Both areas in France and Germany, which were endowed with the coal and iron resources, had voted for the new federal arrangement. It had been carefully explained to them that they would benefit economically and no longer have their lives interrupted on a regular basis by military conflict.

The wives and children in both France and Germany were delighted that this territorial dispute had been resolved peacefully. It had become obvious that this war was destined to last a very long time at the cost of many many lives. They just wanted their husbands and fathers home safely so that they could resume a normal family life. The local mayors organised festivities in the villages and much wine was drunk in the French villages and much beer was drunk in the German villages. There was also much discussion about the memorials which should be erected to honour those who had fought and died in this truncated war.

There were, of course, pockets of virulent resentment at the outcome of the peace talks. In particular amongst those who had fought in the 1870 war. The German veterans were incensed at the loss of Lorraine, which they had acquired after bitter fighting. The French veterans were furious that Alsace was lost forever. Because of the British blockade there had been food shortages in Germany and now riots broke out between those who had opposed war before its outset and those who resented any concessions to the French. In particular those who were opposed to the peace resented intensely Rosa Luxembourg's involvement in the peace process.

Now that the results have been published, Colonel Monash had particular trouble with the German army in Alsace. The senior officers demanded to know why they should continue to retreat from the previous front line now that Alsace had become German territory. Colonel

Monash explained that part of the peace treaty involved the destruction of French and German armaments and future inspections to ensure that neither country was re-arming. He explained that the role of the Spaniards and Scandinavians was as peacekeepers and, that if this involved military action to enforce the peace terms, he would not hesitate to bring in large numbers of Spanish and Scandinavian troops to enforce those terms. He emphasised that the German government had accepted the peace terms, including the destruction of armaments. The German officers grumbled but continued their withdrawal.

Now that the proposal for a federal iron and steel community had been agreed in the voting, Jean Monnet was invited to Nancy to participate in its establishment. He agreed that, as Strasbourg was a border town, it would be a logical headquarters for the new institution. He suggested that the civil servants recruited to administer the institution should all be bilingual. The Constitution of the proposed iron and steel community should be flexible so that in future it might be able to admit other countries into its Federation. This could lay the foundation for a United States of Europe and the elimination of future European wars if it were approached gradually and sensitively. Keynes warned that they would need to take careful heed of the problems which New World federations had had. The USA had had a civil war in which hundreds of thousands had died, Canada had particular difficulties with the French-speaking province of Québec and in Australia there were regular secessionist demands from the west. He wondered how successful a federation between countries with different languages, religions, and much economic, social and cultural diversity could be. This did not deter Monnet, who appeared to have a messianic vision for his

United States of Europe. His plan was to extend it slowly both in terms of scope and depth until the participants found themselves trapped in a supranational institution which was very difficult to leave. Keynes realised that he would have to research carefully the history of previous federations and publish the results in a book. He would call it The Economic Consequences of Jean Monnet.

In Britain and Australia the public response was less equivocal. There was some limited opposition to the outbreak of peace, mainly from groups which were in no danger of personal involvement, because of their age or sex, i.e. veterans of the first Boer War and the "white feather brigade". The vast majority of the British and Australian populations were delighted to have their men home, tempered by a sadness for those who "would lie forever in a foreign field". In Accrington and Rothes there were big celebrations to welcome their men home. The Northern Highlanders made sure that the locals were aware how the kilt had led to Fergus' success with a charming French madame. Inevitably much of the local whisky was consumed and several considered whether it might be worthwhile taking a trip to France wearing the kilt. The women of Accrington were very impressed that Graham had nominated Emmeline Pankhurst as one of the peace negotiators, which then led to five feminist members. They invited Emmeline Pankhurst to visit and address them on her role in the peace process. It was now inevitable that the franchise must extend to all adult women.

Villages and towns throughout Britain gave thought to how the fallen should be memorialised. Lloyd George's actions in strengthening the resolve of the French and German statesman was acknowledged. There was some negative reaction to his removal of General Haig, but this was principally from the military elite and members of the Pall Mall clubs. Members of the general public, and particularly those who had fought in the trenches, applauded the sacking of Haig. Lloyd George was consequently promoted from Chancellor to Prime Minister.

In Melbourne, it was unfortunate that their two stars were absent in London but this did not impede the celebrations. In Richmond it was unfortunate that all the Premier team players were still away in London, but all members of the reserve team were present, and their Collingwood rivals had been invited to join the fun. Samuel Harcourt's parents lived in a big house in the seaside suburb of St Kilda, which included a large Jewish enclave. It was also the home of one of the least successful teams in Melbourne's football league. Because of the involvement of their son and Colonel Monash they decided to throw a big party for all their Jewish friends. Mrs Harcourt advised her husband that, as Rory had been Samuel's companion in the peace process, and that as Samuel was to be Rory's best man, his family should be included in the Jewish festivities. Mr and Mrs Hart were startled when they received the invitation to the party at the Harcourt's. They had never before been invited to a function at what they knew would be such a large and gracious house. They knew little about the Jewish religion, other than that they rejected everything that was written in the New Testament. They felt a little intimidated, but Mrs Hart insisted that they must accept, as it would be extremely rude to refuse such a kind invitation. Lorraine had shared with Rory's mother some of the money given her by the Toorak ladies, so she set off with her children to buy all of them, and herself, smart new clothes for the event. She gave her husband enough money and told him to go and buy himself a smart suit, shirt and shoes. He was accustomed to handing over his wage packet to his wife and was alarmed to have the role reversed, but she explained how she had been given the money by Lorraine.

The Harcourts realised that it would be something of a cultural shock for a family of Gentiles to be in a gathering of Jews, so they decided to introduce them as the parents of Richmond's football club captain, a club which had been spectacularly more successful than their own local team. They would then explain that he had been Samuel's co-conspirator in initiating the peace process. The two daughters were instructed to take charge of, and be very hospitable to, the five Hart children. Many of the guests were concerned about the lack of integration of local Jews into the general community so they saw this as an excellent opportunity to engage with a family of Irish-descendant Protestants, which formed a significant social and political section of Melbourne society. The women in particular were keen to learn about Lorraine and details of the forthcoming wedding in London. They were all at least bilingual and they knew that the Gentile population of Melbourne rarely achieved that status, so they were quite impressed that Lorraine had set about learning French and had had conversation classes with the wives of famous French vintners. The husbands, on overhearing this, wanted to know who the vintners were and where they had their vineyards. Rory had written to his parents explaining that they were to have their honeymoon in Nancy and afterwards to travel south to Chablis and Volnay. There were a few French Jews present and it was clear that there were very impressed with, and in fact quite jealous of, these soon-to-be newlyweds. They explained to the other guests that these were two of the very finest wine villages in France.

The daughters had been explaining various aspects of Jewish culture to the Hart children. They explained that in the synagogue women have to sit apart from the men and that once a month, at the appropriate time, they had to go and have a special bath. It was customary for the family to meet together for a candlelit dinner on the Friday evening. At Passover, which occurred at a similar time to the Christian Easter, they drank quite a lot of wine but had to eat bitter herbs; this was to remind them of the time when their ancestors were enslaved in Egypt. They offered to show them around the house so they could see the dining room where so much of their tradition occurred, and some of the rugs and other belongings which their grandparents had managed to take with them when they fled Russia in the last century. The Hart children were fascinated to see all of this, which was so foreign to their austere, working-class, Protestant life in Richmond. On departure Mr and Mrs Harcourt explained that, when Samuel, Rory and Lorraine were all back from London, they would be invited to Friday night dinner, so that the family could hear all about their adventures. The Harcourts concluded that the night had been a great success and they hoped that Rory and Lorraine would continue to be close friends of their son.

Chapter Five

The Wedding

RORY'S teammates realised that the Ritz was not the place for the raucous Bucks party they had in mind, so they were taking over a local pub for the event. They had been in London long enough to become accustomed to the warm flat beer which was on offer. In fact they preferred it to the French plonk they had been drinking for months.

Vida Goldstein was aware that it had been Samuel who had nominated her for the peace negotiating group and consequently they had become quite friendly in Nancy. He had suggested to Lorraine that she would make an excellent wedding guest so she was now in London for the festivities. She called on Lorraine at the Ritz and Lorraine was fascinated to hear her feminist ideology. Vida believed in strict equality between the sexes and that women should have the opportunity to do anything which men did. She could see no reason why women could not play football if that's what they wished to do. In the wedding ceremony she resented the fact that the father walked the bride down the aisle and agreed to give the woman to the man. Moreover, it was offensive that the bridegroom promised to love, honour and cherish, whilst the bride had to love honour and obey. Vida herself would never agree to obey a man! Having watched Rory in many football games, Lorraine realised that she personally was not built for football, but she did have a couple of beefy neighbours who she knew would relish playing football. She had never thought very much about the wedding ceremony and like many young women had just enjoyed the gowns and the flowers. As her father was 12,000 miles away in Melbourne she had planned to walk down the aisle alone, but she had never thought about what got promised. She discussed it with Rory who just laughed and responded that he had never imagined that he would be able to order such a feisty little bundle about. They visited St-Martin-in-the-Field and explained to the vicar that Lorraine would walk down the aisle unaccompanied and that they will both promise to love, honour and cherish. He was quite surprised, but he was not unaware that there were these women called feminists about. Vida said, when she heard all this, that this was going to be one wedding which she would enjoy.

All the Richmond players had brought their black jumpers, which had yellow sashes, with them to Europe and they intended to wear them when they made a guard of honour for the newly-weds as they left the church. Arsenal football club had been in contact with Ken Stanley and invited all Richmond players to their next match against Tottenham Hotspur. It was explained that Tottenham were the local rivals and so equivalent to Collingwood for Richmond. They were particularly interested to meet Bob Fraser as they had heard he had great potential as a goalie, and perhaps he would like to join in one of the pre-season practice matches? They also enquired if they would be welcome to join in the guard of honour at St-Martin-in-the-Field. Ken immediately accepted both offers, and said that

Bob would be interested in playing with such a famous old club.

Lorraine's wedding gown fitted her small but curvaceous figure snuggly, so the congregation stood in admiration to watch her walk down the aisle alone to the accompaniment of Wagner's Bridal Chorus. The church was packed to overflowing as many London mothers wanted to see the man who had played such a role in perhaps saving their sons' lives. When it came to Lorraine making her wedding vows there were gasps from some of the women in the congregation. Vida Goldstein smiled and resolved to try and speak to some of the unmarried women when they spilled out onto Trafalgar Square. She might just be able to start a movement to get this obnoxious asymmetry removed from the Christian marriage service. Rory looked very handsome in his Henry Buck's suit as Lorraine took his arm to walk up the aisle to Mendelssohn's Wedding March. When they emerged from the church they encountered a guard of honour, first of men dressed in black and gold jumpers, followed by another group dressed in red jumpers. A large group of London mothers and girlfriends milled in the square along with many Arsenal fans who wanted to thank Rory for ensuring that all of their team had come back intact. The mothers and girlfriends wanted to kiss Rory and thank him in person, so he quickly pointed out that his best man Samuel was equally responsible for the survival of their sons and boyfriends, so they set about sharing their kisses with him. Claudette was most amused as the French had an image of the British as reserved and unemotional.

A horse-drawn carriage took the young married couple down Pall Mall and up St James's to the Ritz, where they awaited their guests for the wedding breakfast, which the Ritz was so kindly providing. The reason for their generosity was because it had been feared that their "mother hotel", the Ritz Paris, would be taken over by the Germans if they had ended up victors in this dreadful war. The menu was deliberately French in style: first there was a choice of escargot or cuisses de grenouilles, followed by a choice of confit de canard or boeuf bourguignon, next a choice of Comte, Brie and Bleu de Auvergne cheeses, finally chocolate soufflé or crêpes Suzette. The sommelier had decided it would be appropriate to serve the Chablis and Volnay which Lorraine had ordered on her first evening at the Ritz. Lorraine and Claudette explained to the stunned footballers that they had to begin by eating either snails or frogs' legs. This was a very long way from the grilled lamb chops and boiled vegetables they were accustomed to at home. Peter Wood took the initiative and said that there was no point in being abroad if one did not take the advantage to experience the local food, so he quickly opted for the frogs' legs. After tasting them he explained that they tasted a little bit like chicken, so most of his teammates decided that they would be the safer option. Lorraine suggested to Rory that one of them should order the snails and the other frogs' legs so they could share them and get to experience both. Rory didn't actually fancy eating a snail but he was happy to do anything to please his new bride.

When it came to the second course it was much more straightforward as it amounted to a choice between duck and beef, although they were to be presented in an unfamiliar format. They thought cheese was just cheese, as it came in a homogeneous block at the grocers and was in fact an Australian version of cheddar, so to be presented with this choice of France's most famous cheeses was quite a surprise. The more conservative of them opted for the

Comte, but Peter Wood quickly indicated he wanted to try both the brie and the Blue de Auvergne. Both the soufflé and crêpe proved to be successful deserts and they were impressed with the waiter's skill at making the crêpes.

Rory had explained to them the fallacy which they had fallen into when ordering plonk, so they had been careful not to repeat that in the presence of sommelier. He offered them the choice of the Chabis or Volnay and, whichever they chose, they were startled at how smooth and delicious it tasted compared with the plonk they had been drinking in the trenches. Claudette said that, in view of the sarcastic comments she had heard about British food in France, it was a paradox that the best French meal she had ever had was here in London, so she asked the waiter to pass her French compliments on to the chef. Finally the sommelier offered them a fine cognac or a glass of Grand Marnier. Peter Wood inevitably chose the Grand Marnier. Afterwards the guests departed and left the bridal couple to their honeymoon activities.

The honeymooners did get up after lunch to go for a stroll in Green Park and looked at Buckingham Palace, not knowing that they would be invited in there when they returned from France. In the evening they ate early, as next day they had to get the train and ferry on their way to Paris. They were to spend three evenings at the Paris Ritz before they set off by train to Nancy. The staff at the Paris Ritz were quite surprised that this young Australian woman spoke such good French. They suggested that the Hunters would get more of a flavour of Paris if they ate at some of its famous Brasseries rather than in the Ritz dining room. They were given directions to Saint-Germain and they set off to Les Deux Magots. There had been a collection of art books in the library of the ocean liner on which Lorraine had travelled to England and she had spent hours looking through them. One artist in particular whose work she had loved was Marie Laurencin and she knew that Marie was in the habit of visiting Les Deux Magots with her friend Pablo Picasso, so she was very excited to be eating in a place which Marie frequented. She explained the style of Marie's painting to Rory and he was so impressed that this little ladies hairdresser had such an enquiring mind. He realised that he had a wife who was not just a delicious lover, but also someone who would be able to widen his mind beyond the narrow curriculum he had experienced at Richmond State School.

It was now that Lorraine's knowledge of French came to the fore as none of the waiters spoke any English. She ordered French onion soup and cassoulet as she knew they were famous dishes. She ordered Sancerre from the Loire, as her vintner friends had told her that this was also a fine wine. It was romantic strolling back along Saint-German to the Ritz and they laughed at the fact that Melburnians proudly refer to the "Paris end of Collins Street".

They breakfasted on strong black coffee and pain au chocolat and Rory was amused when Lorraine explained that the French word for breakfast was "the little lunch". It seemed to him that they did eat quite a lot for breakfast. Lorraine explained to the reception staff at the Ritz that she was particularly keen to see paintings by Cezanne, Manet and Laurencin. They knew of Cezanne and Manet, but they knew nothing of Marie. Lorraine chastised them gently for not knowing of a very talented French female artist. They were shamefaced at having to have a young Australian woman instruct them about French painters, so they made some enquiries on the telephone and came back with several galleries they could recommend. They gave Lorraine a Paris Metro map and indicated which stations were closest to these galleries. They set off for the nearby Metro station to experience their first journey on an underground train. Lorraine checked where they would have to change lines and soon they emerged close to the first gallery on her list. To her delight it was displaying one of Cezanne's paintings of Mont Saint Victoire. She explained that this was a beautiful mountain range close to where Cezanne lived and that he had painted it many times. When they arrived at the gallery which was displaying Marie Laurencin's paintings she was delighted that they had her famous painting "Les Jeunes Filles". The third gallery, which had Manet's works, included one of her favourites: "In the Conservatory". Rory had never realised that such beautiful paintings existed and he was so grateful to Lorraine for introducing him to them, but he suggested that it might be time to return to the Ritz and engage in some love-making before dinner. They were getting used to what each other liked and had an energetic time before they dressed for dinner.

They decided to eat at Le Balzar so they travelled on the Metro to Odeon. Both ate escargot and Noix de Saint Jacques, finishing with tarte tatin. A Grand Cru from Saint Emillion was chosen to accompany the food. They walked back along Saint-Germain and Lorraine was thinking how incredibly lucky she was to be able to see such beautiful art, eat such delicious food and smell Paris all because her marvellous husband, along with Samuel, had shown the courage and initiative to set in process the peace talks which had ended a horrible war. When they were eating pain au chocolat next morning, Lorraine said that, as she had chosen their activities yesterday, Rory should choose what they did today. He said that they should visit the famous tourist sights and he knew that the Eiffel Tower and the Arc de Triomphe would be amongst them. Lorraine said that they should add the cathedral of Notre Dame and the Luxembourg Gardens to the list. In the evening he might enjoy seeing some French ladies doing the cancan at the Moulin Rouge. They consulted the Metro map and worked out the most efficient way to visit all these sights. By the time they got to the Moulin Rouge Lorraine was grateful to sit down. She did notice Rory took quite an interest in the ladies' legs, but she knew by now that it was female breasts which most excited him, so she was quietly confident that she presented appropriate erotic attraction for him.

Next morning Lorraine thanked the reception staff for all the help they had been in ensuring she and Rory had had an exciting time in Paris, and then they set off for the Gare de l'Est. Word has got around about their presence in Paris en route to Nancy, so a large crowd of wives and girlfriends were there to bid them bon voyage.

They were to stay at the Grand Hotel de la Reine. It was situated in Nancy's beautiful square, Place Stanislas, with its spectacular golden gates. The city had become famous because of its location for the peace negotiations. In view of Rory's role in establishing these negotiations and in the choice of Nancy for its location, the Grand Hotel was delighted to offer the young couple free accommodation for their honeymoon. When they went down for breakfast Lorraine put on her Cross of Lorraine. This intrigued the waitress so Lorraine explained that Rory had bought it for her previously, because her name was Lorraine and he had decided that this therefore was the appropriate place for a honeymoon. "Oh how romantic, so we have a Lorraine in Lorraine" replied the waitress. "Actually I have just been in Lorraine in Lorraine" said Rory. The waitress blushed and scuttled off to get their coffee and pain au chocolat.

"How are we going to go back to living in a little timber house in Richmond after all this grand living?" said Rory. "I have a surprise for you" was Lorraine's reply, "I have enough money in hand from what the Toorak ladies gave me to put a deposit on a small cottage in Hawthorn". This was the middle-class suburb just across the river from Richmond. "But how will we pay the mortgage, as I haven't finished my apprenticeship as a plumber and I don't get a lot of money from the football club?"

"That's simple. I still have my job at Toorak Ladies."

"But I didn't think that married women worked." was Rory's response. "Not any more, and remember all that I have learned from Vida Goldstein." Rory realised that he had got himself a wife, who was not just intelligent and knowledgeable, but also at the forefront of change in society. He accepted that he would have to live with this, and defend her from any critics she was likely to encounter on her way; not that she wouldn't be perfectly capable of defending herself, but he thought it important that he made it clear that he fully agreed and supported her in her newly acquired feminist position. He resolved to read this book by John Stuart Mill which she had told him about, and hoped that one day soon he would be able to see Ibsen's play The Dolls House.

They spent some of their days exploring the art nouveau delights of Nancy and Rory showed her the Ducal Palace where the negotiations had taken place. Most evenings they ate in Brasserie Excelsoir; inevitably word had got around about who they were, so there was always a steady stream of Lorrains coming up to shake Rory's hand and kiss Lorraine on the cheek. When it came time to leave Lorraine thanked the reception staff at the Grand Hotel profusely, telling them that it had been a perfect location for a honeymoon and that they would be back sometime in the future. There was a crowd at the station to wish them well on their journey south to Dijon where they were to meet Lorraine's vintner friends. First they travelled west to Chablis which was a very pretty little town surrounded by vineyards. Initially they were shown into the cellar which had hundreds of barrels of various vintages. They were invited to taste some of the most famous Grand Cru vintages. Rory found it delicious and such a contrast to the plonk they had been drinking in the trenches that they really shouldn't be called the same product. It was explained to him that French men and women were always well aware of the difference between a Grand Cru Chablis and a Vin Ordinaire. Next they wandered around the vineyard, which was set on steep slopes, and they got an excellent view of the surrounding countryside. The local mayor and other dignitaries had been invited to dinner and naturally they sampled more of the best vintages in the cellar. Next morning they set off south east to Volnay, which was also a beautiful little village. Once again they sampled the best Grand Crus in the cellar and strolled around the vineyard, followed by dinner with the local dignitaries. It was now time to return to London and Lorraine emphasised to her vintner friends that, if they ever were back in Victoria searching land for a vineyard, they must contact her so that she could repay their hospitality.

Chapter Six

Consequences of Peace

AS the German troops withdrew into home territory they encountered a mixed reaction from the locals. Most, who were beginning to suffer from food shortages, were grateful that the war was over and that the British now would presumably lift their blockade. But members of the Freikorps considered that it was treacherous to have made these concessions, and when they heard that it was a Jew called Monash who was overseeing the withdrawal they were enraged. The German officer, who had guarded the little Corporal called Hitler, and finally shot him, recognised the same fanatical xenophobia and anti-Semitism in what these Freikorps enunciated. As the withdrawal continued further into home territory and the destruction of armaments was overseen by Spanish and Scandinavian troops, this xenophobia erupted into violence. The Freikorps considered themselves members of a superior race, and were incensed that a large group of Spanish soldiers were overseeing the decimation of their military equipment. Moreover, they had learned that the Spanish and Scandinavian troops would be remaining in their country, in order to inspect their manufacturing industry to ensure that no replacement armaments were being produced. Their intense resentment inevitably led to rioting in several German cities, where large groups, fuelled by the food shortage, had welcomed the end of hostilities. The Sparticists, a group of radical communists led by Rosa Luxembourg, were the natural enemies of the Freikorps, and they clashed violently in Berlin. Meanwhile the German Navy had mutinied and refused orders to attack the British fleet.

In the midst of all this chaos the Social Democratic Party, which had won 35% of the vote in the recent Parliamentary elections and was led by Haase, who had been one of the peace negotiators, stepped in to attempt to maintain order. They proposed an end to the constitutional monarchy and the displacement of Kaiser Wilhelm. Instead there was to be an elected Republican government and, recognising the importance which the three German feminists had played in the peace process, there would be universal adult suffrage. Also there would be a nationwide campaign to encourage women to stand for the new Parliament. There was to be an end to "kinder, kirche und kuchen". There was a general acceptance of Haase's proposals and Kaiser Wilhelm fled to the Netherlands, thankful that he had not suffered the fate which he feared was awaiting his cousin, the Tzar.

In the election which followed, the Social Democratic party won almost 40% of the vote, so Haase became the first elected President of Germany and, having been impressed by their performance in the peace talks, he appointed the three feminists, Stritt, Luxembourg and Zetkin to senior positions in his cabinet. Max Weber had predicted that the aftermath of the war was going to have a significant impact on European society and here was the first demonstration of that. He was confident that having three such intelligent, articulate and forthright women in senior political positions would stimulate a sexual revolution in German society. Clara Zetkin had been bemused when Haase had invited her to be his Minister for Defence. It did seem inconsistent with her pacifist activity, but he explained that this is exactly why he wanted her in that role, to examine what happened in the past and to keep the military under strict control in the future. He had also done it to provoke the senior military. The Generals worked in an all male environment and the only women in their lives were wives, who accepted their subservient role in the household. The prospect of having to be answerable to a woman raised their blood pressure to dangerous levels.

It began immediately when Clara asked to see all the documents relating to the planning for war and its implementation. They immediately began stonewalling, claiming that it was top secret, for which she did not have clearance. She immediately started giggling and reminded them that she was the Minister for Defence and if she did not get these documents post haste she would not hesitate to replace them with more cooperative officers. "I want them all on my desk in the morning and if any time I discover that there are some missing there will be sackings". Marie and Rosa were delighted when Clara recounted these goings-on so they set off to share a bottle of wine in celebration. Marie had been appointed to a new post as Minister for Women so she outlined to her two friends what action she was intending to take. She intended to take the appropriate legal action to protect women, and one priority was easier access to divorce, and to do away with this archaic nonsense of a marital crime as a necessary basis for divorce. Instead, it should be that the irretrievable breakdown of the marriage could be demonstrated. She intended to tackle domestic violence and to ensure that there were safe refuges where women and children could flee in the face of violence. The police were to be educated about domestic violence and instructed to take it seriously. Female police were to be recruited and to be specially available to deal with rape allegations and any acts of sexual abuse. On the health front she intended to ensure that women had free access to birth control and abortion so that they could be in charge of their own bodies. This would be available to women over 18 without any need for parental permission. She knew that this would make the church apoplectic, but they were going to have to realise that society had changed because of this wretched war and women demanded to be heard. She would also pursue equal opportunity for women in education and employment. Why were there no female doctors or lawyers? Rosa observed that this was a commendable and large agenda so she hoped they would be in office long enough for it to be achieved.

As Rosa was a well respected economist, she was appointed Finance Minister, which had an effect on bankers and leading industrialists equivalent to that which Clara had had on the military elite. Men in the military and in business were going to have to get used to a quite different state of affairs. Likewise the church was going to find its patriarchal values seriously challenged. Marie's equal employment opportunities endeavours could well extend to the church and we could find ourselves with female priests or even female bishops. Even Max Weber was surprised by the pace of change being implemented by these three women.

When Clara arrived at her desk next morning it was as she expected: it was piled high with documents and reports in an obvious attempt at obfuscation. She called in all the Colonels who were present and asked them how keen they were to become Generals. She announced that they could prove their keenness and loyalty by sifting through the pile and reducing it to one which concerned the planning and build up for war, and another which involved decisions about the day-to-day implementation of the war. Then she called in the Generals and told them that if they retaliated in any way upon the Colonels, who were helping her, they would be immediately dismissed. By mid-afternoon the Colonels had reduced the pile of documents to one which was manageable, so Clara set about browsing through them. Early in the evening she came to the letter received by the Kaiser detailing Falkenhayen's plan for a battle of attrition against the French in Verdun. It was very difficult to believe that any human being could so casually commit to the loss of hundreds of thousands of lives. She decided that she must show this document to Rosa immediately, but as she approached the exit a guard blocked her way and explained that she was not authorised to remove documents from the building. She asked who had given him that instruction and when he gave the name of the responsible General she returned to the building and ordered that all the Generals present assemble in her office. She immediately announced that the responsible General was forthwith dismissed and that if any other General dared to impede her actions and challenge her authority they also would be immediately dismissed. Rosa had been extremely vigorous in pursuing peace and had formed an alliance with Jean Jaurès in that quest. It was decided that the contents of this document should be immediately disclosed to all the European people and they decided that Louise Mack would be the appropriate person to do so. It was Louise who had informed the public about the horrors of trench warfare and the lethal existence which the troops endured.

Marie decided that abortion and birth control would be her first priority. When she announced in parliament that any legal impediment to them was to be abolished, and that they were to be available free with the state paying the cost, there was uproar from the right wing and religious press. They thundered on about an assault on Christian values and the encouragement of promiscuity. She replied that the existence of state sanctioned brothels carried the implication that promiscuity was acceptable for men, but now they're trying to say that it's not acceptable for women. Had they not noticed that the Minister for Defence and the Minister for Finance currently were women. Differential treatment for men and women was now a thing of the past and the sooner they recognised it the better. She warned that any type of direct action aimed at denying women access to birth control or abortion would be dealt with severely.

Rosa's first action at the Ministry of Finance was to ask them to convene a meeting with all those industrialists who had engaged in the production of armaments. When they met she explained that, as a courtesy, she was advising them ahead of a public announcement in parliament that their companies were to be nationalised without compensation as a punishment for their contribution to this dreadful war. Rosa then instructed senior civil servants in her department immediately to begin an investigation into what peacetime production could be undertaken with the equipment and factories which were to be nationalised. She also instructed that the workforce was to be unionised and that recognised independent trade union leaders were to conduct this process.

Misogynistic hysteria dominated the pages of the press: " challenging military authority", "encouraging promiscuity and immorality", "nationalising key industries". So it was decided that a new daily paper would be produced under the supervision of Louise Mack. It would be called "Half Our Society" and it would explain that human families were not like a pack of lions, nor a family of gorillas; there was no logical need for a dominant male "head of household" with a subservient obedient wife. That was a construct of religion (actually embedded in the Christian wedding service): religion which was based on superstition and not on science. Why did you have to have a penis in order to be a surgeon, a judge, a general, an engineer or even a vicar?

In many households there was an attempt to ban the purchase and reading of this pernicious publication. But now, thanks to the reporting by Louise Mack of male decision-making in the recent war, female members of the households refused to be intimidated. There was much grumbling in the beer halls, but Marie Stritt's strictures about domestic violence and retraining of the police force meant that they did have to acquiesce in the changed power situation within the household.

Initially Fritz and Wilhelm had encountered a mixed reception when they returned home. Those who were glad the war was over and that food shortages were diminishing saw them as saviours, but the Freicorps considered them traitors, and they had to be protected from assassination. Clara's revelations about the huge loss of life which would have been incurred if the war had continued ensured that Fritz and Wilhelm were considered heroes, and there was overwhelming support for the campaign launched by "Half Our Society" for them to be awarded the high German honour: "Pour le Merit". Haase was well aware of their importance in establishing the peace negotiations and readily agreed that they should be honoured in this way. He awarded the honour in person and also implemented a Parliamentary regulation that at the age of 50 they should be awarded a generous lifetime pension.

Meanwhile Clara had been pursuing her policy of demilitarisation. To accompany the destruction of armaments, she set about disbanding the reserve army and abolishing conscription. Members of the reserve army were to surrender immediately any military equipment which they possessed, and they were warned that they would be prosecuted if they engaged in any paramilitary activities in the future. From now on Germany was to have only a small professional army. She knew that equivalent action would be taken in France so there was no danger in having just a small professional army.

In France there was significant opposition to the troop withdrawal by a substantial proportion of the population, which resented the permanent loss of Alsace and were unhappy about having to share their valuable iron resources within the new supranational iron and steel community. There had been a long history of conflict between France and Spain and the presence of Spanish troops enforcing the withdrawal and overseeing the systematic destruction of armaments inflamed those opposing the peace settlement. Anti-Semitism was not absent in France and the fact that one of the initiators of the whole peace process was an Australian Jew called Harcourt, that a prominent member of the peace negotiating team had been the German Jew, Rosa Luxembourg, and that moreover the implementation of the peace process was being overseen by a German Jew called Monash added to the outrage. Some even predicted that the permanent presence of Spanish troops on French soil, inspecting their manufacturing industry to ensure there was no clandestine production of armaments, could lead to a renewal of the Peninsula war. When Colonel Monash heard of this, he ensured that a majority of the troops performing these functions in France were the Scandinavians. Pierre was persona non grata and had to flee to Spain.

Poincaré felt intimidated by this opposition to the peace agreement and decided that, given his diplomatic expertise, it would make sense to appoint Cambon as his Minister for Defence. He took a rather more diplomatic route than Clara Zetkin was taking in Germany; nevertheless he ensured that conscription was abolished and that the reserve army was stood down and stripped of its military equipment. He explained to the Generals that, because of the action he had just taken, and the fact that in future the German army was to be restricted to a small defence force, there would not be the need for anywhere near as many military in the senior command, and so he was offering them generous resignation terms which would include an honourable discharge. He explained that because comparable arrangements were being implemented in Germany and because the British had never had a reserve army of conscripts there was no danger in this for the French State.

Louise Mack had ensured that a large number of copies of the first issue of "Half Our Society", which contained full details of Falkenhayen's Plan for a war of attrition in Verdun, were available to the French public. This had an immediate impact on the French attitude to the peace outcome. The women suddenly realised that there had been a high probability that they would have ended up as widows trying to support several fatherless children. The men realised that they would have endured many more months in the trenches followed most likely by death.

The fact that the Minister for Defence and the Minister for Finance in Germany were now women and that there was a new post, the Minister for Women, staggered the women of France. There had been Australian, British and German feminists as members of the peace negotiating team but not one from France. They were, of course, pleased that Marie Curie had been a member of the negotiating team, but she was a brilliant scientist not a political operator. Consequently, French women adopted a much more militant stance and demanded that they have the vote immediately. They also demanded that they have a much more prominent role in public life akin to what had happened in Germany; otherwise they would campaign for an extension of the iron and steel community into a closer form of Federation with the Germans. They did not see why they should have an inferior position in public life compared to the women in their German neighbour. Poincaré had had weeks to observe the behaviour of the five militant feminists during the peace negotiations. Consequently he was well aware that women were intelligent, articulate and determined. He had long been aware, because of Marie Curie's achievements, that women could be super intelligent and super industrious. He decided to consult Cambon about how to respond to these challenges.

Cambon recommended that French women over the age of 21 should immediately have the vote, otherwise he would face months, if not years, of serious social unrest. He also recommended that women be appointed to head at least two ministries, one of which would be a ministry for women's affairs. "If we are too far out of line with our German neighbour this will cause serious and ongoing resentment and unrest amongst most of our female population, but if you act immediately you will at least maintain the ministries of defence and finance in male hands". Poincaré decided to take this advice and immediately recommended to the National Assembly that they legislate for universal adult suffrage. He decided to appoint a woman to be Head of the Ministry of Health and to established a Ministry for Women with, of course, a woman as head. Olga Petit was a highly regarded avocat so she was appointed Minister for Women. Madeleine Bres, who was the first woman in France to obtain a medical degree, was appointed Minister for Health. Both women were astonished, but delighted, to be offered these posts and readily accepted them. Olga immediately set off to Berlin to liaise with Marie Stritt and to learn of any opposition she was encountering. She returned intending to take equivalent action to Marie except that the issues of health would more appropriately be implemented by Madeleine Bres.

Thanks to Clara Zetkin's revelations about the Falkenhayen plan, the majority of the French population were now grateful to have a peace settlement and there was public guilt that Pierre had been forced to flee to Spain. Cambon went in person to apologise on behalf of the French nation and invite him back so that he could experience the approbation which he deserved. A large public rally was to be arranged in the Place de la Concorde so that the public would have the opportunity to demonstrate their gratitude to him. Afterwards he was invited to the Elysée Palace to receive the award of Chevalier of the Legion d'Honneur.

Olga's first action was to ensure that there was appropriate recognition for Marie Curie. Olga was expecting that Marie would have many more years to perform her scientific research, but when ultimately she did die it was to be established now that her remains would be interred in the Pantheon. There had never been the remains of a woman interred in the Pantheon and it was obviously appropriate that Marie Curie should be the first. In the villages there was much discussion about how the French troops who had died in this war should be memorialised. Most villages had one or two fatalities although the odd one had none and the unfortunate ones had five or six. It was generally agreed that a small stone pedestal should be erected with the names of the fallen engraved on it. In some villages it was also suggested that there should be another pedestal with the names of the six who had initiated the peace negotiations engraved on it. There was opposition to this on the basis that only one was French and moreover two were German. The counter argument was put that if it hadn't been for these six the other little pedestal would have been a tower. So it was resolved that each village would have two pedestals.

Madeleine and Olga faced the same battery of opposition as Marie had encountered in Germany. In this case it was in the cafés where men congregated to exchange their grievances. Some feared that equal opportunity in education and employment for women would lead to them losing their own jobs, whereas others feared that they might end up having to work for a female boss. Madeleine and Olga had both been the first female members of their professions in France, and had struggled to get there, so it was to be a priority that they would open up the employment market to women. The men speculated about what would happen if someday in the future, when they had to consult a doctor about some sexual disease only to discover it was a woman! When they raised this hypothetical situation with their wives they were laughed at. "What do you think happens when we are pregnant or have a breast lump?" Madeleine announced similar health provisions to those Marie had introduced in Germany and, predictably, French men, who were accustomed to visiting brothels, railed against the encouragement this would give to their daughters to be promiscuous.

Emmeline Pankhurst's role in the peace process was well recognised in the British press, and the Manchester Guardian, in particular, scorned the past behaviour of those who had opposed granting the franchise to women. In edition after edition, leader writers argued that the opponents of female franchise should be utterly ashamed of themselves for the treatment suffragettes had suffered at the hands of the state. They argued that there should be a state apology and compensation for all those who had been imprisoned simply for demanding a right which would be expected in any democratic state. If London was not to be the misogynistic capital of Europe female franchise must be granted immediately and women encouraged to stand at what must be an imminent general election. Regardless of which party gained a majority they should ensure that at least two women were appointed to senior Cabinet posts.

Louise Mack had ensured that a large number of copies of Half Our Society were sent to Britain and it reinforced the Manchester Guardian's demands. The contents of Half Our Society, and the news of the current role of women in the political life of France and Germany, encouraged many British women to be supportive of the feminists' demands. They were now aware how important an international group of feminists had been in ensuring a peace settlement, which meant that their menfolk were coming home safely.

With very great reluctance the politicians at Westminster accepted that they could not be out of line with France and Germany, so they extended the franchise to all citizens over the age of 21 and dissolved parliament so that a general election could take place. Emmeline Pankhurst and Millicent Fawcett were both elected with substantial majorities. Emmeline was appointed to head the new Ministry for Women and Millicent was appointed as Minister for Health.

One of Emmeline's first actions was to stop the universities of Cambridge and Oxford refusing to admit women to their degrees. Consistent with feminist theory she was following a similar line to Marie and abolishing "marital crime" as the pathway to divorce and instead substituting evidence of the irretrievable breakdown of the marriage. One of Millicent's first actions was to raise the age of consent and abolish child marriage. She also repealed The Contagious Disease's Act which imposed strict conditions on prostitutes and included provision for imprisonment, but did not apply to the men who had been responsible for the prostitutes' infection.

As Graham Blakey had initiated the practice of appointing feminists to the peace negotiating panel, he was much revered amongst the feminist community and there were calls for him to receive an appropriate civilian honour. So, along with Angus MacDonald, the Scottish member of the six, he went to Buckingham Palace to be awarded the CBE. Australia also awarded Imperial honours so there was some discussion about whether Rory and Samuel should also be included in this award ceremony. The private secretary to King George the Fifth explained discreetly to the Press that the King intended to award a very high honour to the Australian pair in a private ceremony and invite them afterwards for luncheon with Queen Mary. It followed that Rory and Samuel received large envelopes containing gilt-edged invitations to attend the Palace with wife or fiancée for a private ceremony and luncheon. When Samuel received his invitation he rang the King's private secretary to make sure that the four of them would be appropriately dressed for the occasion. The private secretary informed him about dress and recommended that they arrive 30 minutes ahead of time so that they could be instructed on how they should address the King and Queen. Golda's mother took her to Harrods to buy an appropriate dress, while Lorraine chose one from her Collins Street collection.

When they arrived at the Palace the private secretary explained to them that they were both to receive the Order of Merit and he explained how senior and exclusive it was. In future they would be able to put after their name the initials 0M, so that Rory, for instance, would be Rory Hunter 0M. Golda, who knew the most about the British honours system, was very impressed and knew that the guests at her forthcoming wedding would be delighted that her husband had received this award. Fortunately the wedding invitations had not yet been printed, so they would now announce that she was marrying Samuel Harcourt 0M. They were ushered into a small chamber to meet the King and Queen and they did the appropriate bowing and curtsying in which they had been instructed. The King began by pinning the Order of Merit on their jackets and shaking their hands. He then spoke to Lorraine and Golda and said that they must be proud to have two such gallant men as husband or husband to be. Next they moved into an adjacent dining room and the six of them sat down to a delicious luncheon, which began with foie gras.

Queen Mary knew of the art nouveau fame of Nancy so she was keen to ask Rory and Lorraine about their honeymoon there. When they had finished Queen Mary took Lorraine and Golda off to her sitting room so that the men can settle down to cognac and cigars. When the King offered Rory a cigar he explained that, as he was a serious athlete he didn't smoke anything, and he was sure he would choke if he smoked that big thing the King was offering. George the Fifth laughed and said he was glad to see that Rory's athleticism didn't deny him a glass of good French wine followed by some cognac.

The King explained that he had a very personal reason for meeting and honouring them. His cousin the Tzar had been enduring serious civil unrest for some time, and they would know that his other cousin, Kaiser Wilhelm, had been forced to flee to the Netherlands, so naturally he had been nervous that, if this wretched war had dragged on, it was possible that there might have been some serious anti-monarchist unrest in Britain. Consequently he personally had a great debt to the instigators of a peaceful resolution to this war. There were regular luncheons for members of the Order of Merit, but they would be difficult to attend if you were living 12,000 miles away, so he invited them to contact him whenever they were in London and he would arrange a private luncheon for them.

The Arsenal players had been playing host to their Richmond counterparts and explained they were so grateful to Rory as all of their players who had been in the trenches had returned home unscathed. All the Richmond players and Samuel were invited to their next match against Tottenham Hotspur, but when they realised that one of them was called Samuel there might be a problem. He was most likely Jewish and therefore inevitably a Tottenham fan, and would have to sit elsewhere in the stadium. "What for?" asked the Richmond players in unison. "We always separate the fans of competing clubs," was the answer. "What a strange thing to do, we would never do that in Australia," said Ken Stanley. "Okay, we'll make an exception this once but it will be diplomatic if Samuel refrains from applauding any success of Tottenham." Arsenal won 2-1 so the players were in good spirits when the Richmond team visited them in their dressing room.

Lorraine contacted the Countess on the phone number she had been given, and when her butler told her there was a phone call from what sounded like an Australian woman, the Countess hurried to the phone and said that she had read in the papers that Rory has been awarded the Order of Merit. It was a very distinguished honour and Rory had certainly deserved it. She then invited them for dinner five evenings hence and she assured Lorraine that her Major son would be there to thank Rory in person. When Lorraine and Rory arrived at the Countess's home in Belgravia she introduced them first to her husband the Earl of Holborn and her son, then next to the Australian High Commissioner. She also explained that she had invited some of her friends who are sympathetic to the feminist movement. The Major explained to Rory that middle ranking officers, like Captains and Majors, had been in a very awkward situation in the trenches. On the one hand they had been well aware of the misery and danger involved and the reckless disregard for human life being ordered by the senior Generals at military headquarters; on the other hand military discipline meant that they had to apply the orders of the senior Generals. Consequently they had been delighted when the private soldiers and junior officers had taken the action to achieve a peaceful outcome.

The Australian High Commissioner explained that there had been a lot of discussion in Canberra about what would be appropriate honours for Rory and Samuel, but now the King had resolved it by awarding them very distinguished honours. Lorraine replied that two Australian women had played an important role in the achievement of peace in Europe. Vida Goldstein had been an important member of the peace negotiating team and Louise Mack had been important in bringing to the world the horror and futility of this wretched war, so the government should give careful thought to how they should be honoured. The High Commissioner promised to relay her request onto the Australian Prime Minister.

The ladies present had heard about the wedding and there was a rumour that Lorraine intended to go back to work as a ladies hairdresser despite the fact that she was married, and moreover her husband was fully supportive about this unusual behaviour. Lorraine suggested that they might like to meet her new friend, Vera Goldstein, and she recommended that they read John Stuart Mill's famous book on female emancipation.

The Major had spent many months in the trenches so Rory was interested to hear from him how the whole battle of Ypres had developed. It was clear that there had been many many incidents like the one which Rory had complained about. British troops had been trained to obey orders "to do as they were told", so that is why there was so much outrage when a mob of colonials had challenged the system.

The Countess explained to Lorraine that at dinner she was to be seated next to the Earl; he was a notorious old flirt and he had heard how pretty she was, so he wanted to monopolise her over dinner. "But don't worry, he's harmless". The Earl had a great interest in art and was pleased to hear about Lorraine's expeditions to Parisian galleries. He knew little about Marie Laurencin so Lorraine explained enthusiastically why Marie was one of her favourites. He promised that, on his next trip to Paris, he would diligently investigate her work and possibly buy one of her paintings, in which case Lorraine must come to visit on her next trip to London.

Lorraine explained that she had brought her camera so would he mind if she took some photos to take back to show her friends in Melbourne. The Earl agreed on the proviso that one of them was of the two of them together. The butler was then instructed to take several photos of the dinner and particularly one close up with Lorraine. After dinner the Countess enquired if the Earl had been too much of a nuisance. "Oh no, he reminded me of my father," was Lorraine's reply.

"Please don't tell him that, as it would crush his ego," said the Countess. When they were leaving the Countess explained that they had an open invitation to visit them whenever they were in London. Lorraine explained that the Earl had already extended such an invitation, especially if he had managed to buy a Laurencin when he was in Paris. "I guess that's a variation from etchings," sighed the Countess.

Chapter Seven

The Iron and Steel Community

BELGIUM, Luxembourg and the Netherlands had been having some discussions about whether they could combine as a common unit and have uniform customs arrangements. They were all small countries with small populations and they felt that if they combined as an economic unit they would have more power in the European economy. For this reason the proposed iron and steel community was of interest to them so they approached Jean Monnet to enquire if they might possibly join in this arrangement. He explained that this was consistent with his ultimate objective, but at the moment the arrangement was specifically related to the peace treaty, so first he would have to consult the French and German governments. He suggested that they should go ahead and form some customs union amongst themselves, or perhaps a formal Federation of their three countries. He said that in the future this could be integrated with the iron and steel community and perhaps extended to establish a Federation of the five countries.

Meanwhile Maynard Keynes had set to examining the history of federations and the necessary conditions for success. Australia had only recently been federated so he thought this was a good place to start. He discovered that during the 19th century there had been little enthusiasm for Federation from several of the six colonies that existed on the continent and there had had to be several conventions to arrive at a proposal to put to a referendum. The first referendum on Federation failed and one significant issue was rivalry between Melbourne and Sydney about the location of the capital. This was resolved by the strange proposal to establish a new city isolated in sheep country over 100 miles south west of Sydney. He also discovered that between 1823 and 1841 there had been a Federation of several of the Central American countries but it had ended up in Civil War. There had been a short lived Federation between Peru and Bolivia also early in the 19 century. Panama, Colombia and a part of Northwest Brazil had been in a Federation for five years in the middle of the 19th century. The fact that all the countries involved in these failed federations spoke a common language and had a common religion had not ensured success.

He put this historical research together with his knowledge of the Civil War in the United States of America and the problem which the Canadian government had with the Québécois to make a set of recommendations to Jean Monnet. Any federal union of European states should be confined to a group of countries which were at a broadly similar stage of economic development and shared similar social, political and cultural values. It should be a loose Federation of nations without a great deal of power ceded to the federal authority, whose basic role would be to act as a coordinating body and not to impose its authority on member states. This was a much more modest proposal than Monnet's messianic vision for a United States of

Europe, but Keynes considered that it was one with a more realistic prospect of longevity. He recommended that the countries which fitted these criteria were Austria, Belgium , Denmark, France, Germany, Luxembourg and the Netherlands.

There were fundamental economic, social and political differences between the countries of northern Europe and those of the Mediterranean south. Spain was a poorly developed agricultural country which itself had problems because of its federal structure, especially with the region of Catalonia and the Basque country. Italy was politically unstable and had a major problem of internal diversity between the prosperous industrialised north and the impoverished agricultural south. The Balkan countries had been involved in serious internal conflict for centuries, principally because of their religious diversity. Greece had a history of political and financial instability. If any of these countries were included with the above seven in a federal body he foresaw inevitable conflict between the north and south of Europe.

Chapter Eight

Consequences of Peace in Australia

IN Victoria there were some rumblings in the Melbourne Club about not having given the Huns the thrashing they deserved. They would have been too concentrated on reading the financial pages of the newspapers to have bothered with Louise Mack's graphic descriptions, first of the war itself and later of the successful involvement of two Victorians in the achievement of peace. The general public had read Louise's articles and were pleased to hear that their menfolk would soon be on-board ship heading home.

A big welcome home ceremony for Rory, Samuel, Vida, Louise and Colonel Monash was organised in the Melbourne Cricket Ground. The fact that two of them were Jewish did not go unnoticed in the local Jewish community and confirmed their recognition that this was a country with only minimal anti-Semitism. Rory said that he was looking forward to kicking some more goals for Richmond and doing what he could to support the cause of feminism. He intended to call on Henry Bucks to thank them in person for the fine wardrobe they had donated. Samuel said that he was looking forward to returning to the University of Melbourne for his history studies and that perhaps in future centuries he and Rory would at least rate a footnote in any volume written on the 20th century. Vida said it had been a privilege and an inspiration to meet senior members of the British and German feminist groups. They had been impressed to learn that Australian women had had the vote almost from the outset of Federation, but she was aware that the vote was only a foundation on which there was much to build, to ensure that Australian women had complete equality in economic and social life. Louise said she had been proud to report on the crucial activities of four Victorians in the successful achievement of peace. Colonel Monash said that he'd been proud to lead the Australian troops and he respected their independent approach to battle. The master of ceremonies congratulated Rory and Samuel on having been awarded the Order of Merit. He then went on: "I hope that Vida, Louise and Colonel Monash will also get appropriate recognition for their role in bringing this European conflict to an end." Because of Louise's reporting, they all knew the role of Waltzing Matilda in helping to initiate the Christmas truce so now. "Once a jolly swagman camped by a billabong......" was boomed out across Melbourne by 70,000 voices.

Vida set off on a nationwide tour, with copies of Half Our Society, to communicate the inroads into political life being made by women in Europe. Whenever she addressed a public meeting, large numbers of women, and a few men, attended to hear her experience of meeting eminent European feminists and what they were achieving. To date no women have been elected to the Australian parliament, let alone appointed to head major government ministries, so in all six states of the Federation the local feminists resolved that they should certainly stand for the Senate and they would also consider which might be sympathetic electorates for the House of Representatives. In the election which followed shortly, the feminist alliance successfully had one member elected to the Senate in each of the six States. They were also successful in two House of Representatives electorates: one in Melbourne and the other in Sydney. The National party decided that it would be politically expedient to accept a loose coalition with the feminists, so they offered ministries to Vida Goldstein and Edith Cowin. Edith was made Minister for Health and Vida was appointed to head a new Ministry for Women. Edith quickly moved to ensure that birth control and abortion were available to all women and that sex education was taught in all schools. Vida introduced specific laws to deal with domestic violence and recommended that the various state police forces were trained how to deal with it and to take it very seriously. She next acted to remove any impediments to women's access to education or employment, and instructed that all public bodies must immediately open up employment to women. One outcome was that when the Melbourne and Metropolitan Tramways Board approached the leader of the Tramway Union, Desmond O'Shea, to accept having female conductors on the trams, he agreed on the condition that their pay was exactly the same as the men's. So this notoriously militant trade union leader was the first person in the country to ensure equal pay for equal work. Many of these actions taken by the two feminists were in areas where the authority belonged to the States. It was explained to them that they had the option of complying with these federal directives or there would be referenda which would give the populace the right to decide if power over policing, education and health should be transferred to the federal government. All six States preferred to implement what Edith and Vida were requiring, rather than risk losing control of these important areas.

Because of his crucial role in delivering successfully the terms of the peace agreement, Colonel Monash was made a Knight Grand Cross of the Order of the Bath. Vida and Louise were both awarded the Companion of Honour (CH). Richmond Town Council was proud to have a resident who was instrumental in peacemaking and had been awarded the Order of Merit by King George the Fifth, so they decided that he should be awarded the freedom of the city.

Lady Bailey organised a big social event in her Toorak mansion so that they could hear full details of Lorraine's wedding and travels. Some were envious of her experience dining at the Captain's table, others were envious of her experience at the two Ritzes, one in London and one in Paris. In particular they wished their honeymoon had been in Nancy. A couple of the men were particularly interested to hear about the vineyards and cellars they had visited in Chablis and Volnay. Lorraine had brought with her photos of the evening she and Rory had spent in Belgrave Square. When she explained that the man with her in the close-up was the Earl of Holborn, they all wanted to know what he was like: "lecherous but harmless" was her reply. Of course they all wanted to hear about her visit to Buckingham Palace and luncheon with King George the Fifth and Queen Mary. They had read Louise Mack's account of the wedding and were most interested to hear how she had got the idea to cherish rather than to obey Rory. She explained that she had learnt a great deal from Vida Goldstein and consequently had developed a feminist position. Rory was fully supportive and agreed with Vida that women should not be denied the right to do anything which men did. Though he did wonder whether they could cope with the rigours of playing football. Lorraine replied but she had seen a soccer match between Arsenal and Tottenham, and she did notice that, because they couldn't use their hands, they often let the ball strike them on the chest and "I'm sure that would be a bigger deterrent for women playing soccer".

Lorraine returned to work at Toorak Ladies Haute Coiffure and began searching for a house in Hawthorn which they could afford. She discovered that a pretty little Edwardian cottage was for sale in a tree-lined avenue off Lisson Grove. It had a large garden at the back so she would be able to have the dog which she had always coveted. Hawthorn was another of Richmond's opponents in the football league, so some of the neighbours were rather taken aback when the Richmond football captain moved in. Samuel and Golda had invited them several times to Friday night family dinners, so when the cottage was set up they were Lorraine and Rory's first guests.

Meanwhile Peter Wood and Paddy Guinness had been planning a strategy to have it established that there would be a referendum on whether Australia should remain in the British Empire or become an independent republic like the United States of America. They received support from most of the troops who had returned from France and had experienced the condescension of British army officers. The Irish catholic population was virtually unanimous in its support. The Scots had long been agitating for independence, so their diaspora in Australia also welcomed the idea of removing the shackles of Empire.

The Nationalist party, pragmatic as ever, realised that there was an inevitability about this request, so they passed the appropriate legislation for a referendum in which the electorate could choose whether to retain the status quo or to sever the link with the British Empire, and replace the British-appointed Governor General with a President elected by the people of Australia. If the referendum was successful, it followed that there would have to be a new national flag and national anthem. The women of Australia knew of the great struggle which British women had had in achieving the right to vote and the horrible treatment which the suffragettes had incurred in that struggle. Consequently they had no desire to retain membership of an organisation which had such reactionary, misogynistic and undemocratic practices in its lead institution.

A coalition of returned soldiers, Scots and Irish descendants whose forebears had campaigned and/or fought for independence from England, and women who were disgusted by the behaviour of the British parliament in denying the franchise to women ensured that the referendum passed comfortably: 61% to 39%. Colonel Monash was pressed to enter the race to be Australia's first president, Waltzing Matilda was chosen as the new national anthem and Margaret Preston was commissioned to design a new national flag. Colonel Monash graciously declined the request that he stand to be President of the new Republic. He explained that he was accustomed to living in a big city with a diverse population so he could not imagine living in a small town in a remote location with a population of politicians, civil servants and journalists.

Chapter Nine

1925

TEN years on from the peace settlement, life had returned to normal so celebrations and memorial services were planned to mark this anniversary. The war had been fought on French territory so it was their agriculture and industry which had been damaged. The German Defence Minister, Clara Zetkin, had suggested to young German men, who no longer had to spend two years as army conscripts, that they might like to spend some of that time volunteering to assist in the repair and reconstruction of the French economy. Many, who were extremely grateful not to have to spend two years in the army, did respond to her request and went off to help repair the damage the French had incurred. As a quasi-federal body was starting to emerge in northern Europe, it would also be valuable to take the opportunity to learn to speak French. So gangs of combined French and German young men, now both freed from conscripted army services, worked to repair the damage done to French agricultural land by artillery fire and the digging of trenches. Rosa Luxembourg had nationalised some major German manufacturers and, once she had established what damage had been done to

French industry, she set them to work to help ameliorate the damage. As with the young Germans working on the land in northern France, this was all done on a voluntary basis and with care not to stress Germany industry.

There had been negotiations between Austria,Belgium, Denmark, France, Germany, Luxembourg and the Netherlands about expanding the iron and steel community into a loose form of customs union. There had been difficulties in achieving free trade within this group of seven: the French did not want tariff-free importation of Dutch cheese or butter, the Germans did not want Belgian beer or Danish bacon to come in tariff-free. Both countries took a protectionist stance, so, when it had been mooted that the group could be expanded geographically, France resisted inclusion of Spain because it feared competition from Spain's wine and olive oil. Italy's entry was also resisted because the French feared competition from the Italian fashion industry. Germany also had rejected Italy's request to join because it feared competition from Italian car manufacturers. Jean Monnet's vision of a United States of Europe was not getting off to a good start. It had been finally resolved that they would be free trade within the confines of the seven , but there would be substantial tariff barriers to protect the seven from external competition.

This meant that Australian butter, lamb, beef and wool had now faced these barriers to European trade. The Australian Ambassador had requested an urgent meeting with the French President. She reminded him that in 1914 Australian troops had come 12,000 miles to support the French against a German invasion; moreover it was Australians who had played a major role in achieving peace, thus saving hundreds of thousands of European lives. Now the French had joined a trade block, which meant that they provided favourable trade terms to their old enemy the Germans, whilst at the same time creating significant trade barriers to their old ally the Australians. The French had the audacity to refer to Britain as "perfidious Albion" but hereinafter Australians would always refer to France as "perfidious Francia". Needless to say, the Australian Ambassador had achieved neither success nor apology from the French President. She had advised the Australian government that they should act immediately to cease all imports of French wine and that Italian and Spanish, instead of French, be taught in Australian schools. She also suggested that Australians holidaying in Europe should consider visiting Madrid and Rome rather than Paris.

Louise Mack had learned full details of this from the Australian ambassador and she ensured that her report was covered extensively in the French newspapers. Very many French men and women were aware of the debt they owed to the Australians in the recent war. In fact most of them lived in villages that had a pedestal which included the names of Australian peacemakers. Fergus' lover renamed her cafe: "Cafe des Australians". Consequently the European customs union had began life with some of its population quite antagonistic to its policies.

Women had made great strides towards equality in society over the decade. There had been three elections to the British House of Commons during that time and, as now at least 50% of the eligible voters were women, this had ensured that approximately one third of the members of the House of Commons were women. They were now well represented in the Cabinet and had some senior portfolios such as Home Secretary and Minister for Education. There were female consultants in many medical specialities, such as haematology and neurology, and they were also well represented at the bar. Women also worked as electricians, carpenters and plumbers. Women's football clubs have been established and major teams such as Arsenal and Liverpool now had sister clubs. Female jockeys had been successful in some of the major races such as the Cheltenham Gold Cup. Even the BBC had responded to the feminist surge and now women were reading the news. On the other hand men were being encouraged to train as nurses, nursery school and primary school teachers, so that there could be a better sex balance in these occupations.

In Germany, Clara Zetkin had opened up the military academies to women and encouraged them to train as officers. So ten years on there were female Majors and Colonels in the German army and female officers in the German Navy. Initially there was consternation when there were meetings of European Finance ministers, or of World Finance ministers, because they were not accustomed to having a woman in their presence, and had always presumed that the female mind could not cope with such complexities. Rosa soon put their minds at rest, as they realised she had a deeper understanding of the complexities of the economic and financial system than they did. She had become concerned about the excesses of the stock market, particularly in the United States of America. She had consulted with Maynard Keynes and they both agreed that there needed to be some regulation of financial markets, but they could not get support from the world's finance ministers who were committed to laissez faire.

When Olga Petit encountered opposition to French women being accepted into military academies she reminded the Generals of Jeanne d'Arc and La Liberté in Delacroix's famous painting. French men were surprised to find that female doctors were not only competent but more empathetic than their male counterparts. They did however chastise them for drinking cognac or pastis for breakfast.

In Australia Vida Goldstein had become accustomed to negotiating with the six States when legislative authority belonged to them rather than the Federal Government. Some of the States had the practice of sacking women if they married, so she quickly put an end to that. Most States did not permit women to enter public bars in hotels and instead insisted that they drink in a "ladies lounge". Vida considered this a caste system akin to what happened in the American south so she insisted it must end.

Graham Blakey stood for the seat of Accrington in the British parliamentary elections and the women, who admired his support for Emmeline Pankhurst, ensured that he was elected as the member for Accrington, which would have given great pleasure to his father. The Scottish people were proud that the Northern Highlanders had honoured the "auld alliance" and gone to the defence of France. In particular they were proud that Angus MacDonald had been one of the six who had initiated the peace process, so on his return Angus was given the freedom of the city of Edinburgh. Fergus decided to spend his demobilisation pay on a Buchanan tartan kilt to enliven his planned regular trips to France. It was one of the most colourful tartans and, on his first trip to the old battlefield, Madame was particularly excited and quickly got one of her best bottles of wine out of the cellar.

When Rory's football career ended he was approached to stand for the Richmond electorate in the State Parliament. His reputation both as a footballer and peacemaker ensured him an easy victory. He set about supporting Vida

Goldstein's campaign for sexual equality in education and employment. He objected to the fact that in the state schools the girls had to learn cooking while the boys had to learn woodwork, so he had it established that both sexes had the right to choose which of these subjects they would pursue. Likewise on the sports field girls had the opportunity to play football and cricket if they so chose. To support Vida's campaign for women to be able to drink in the public bars of hotels he made a point of taking Lorraine into the public bar of the local hotel. When the men grumbled, and muttered that she would just have to put up with their swearing, she replied that there was nothing they could say that she didn't hear on a regular basis from her husband. When anyone, especially journalists, queried why a man was pursuing so many feminist objectives he referred them to John Stuart Mill's Subjection of Women. Rory was also active coaching the Richmond Women's team, which was determined to emulate the success of their male counterpart.

Lorraine had established her own hairdressing salon in the Hawthorn High Street: "Hawthorn Ladies Haut Coiffure". It was within walking distance from home which made a difference from having to catch two trams. Because of Lorraine's reputation she soon had customers coming from three surrounding suburbs and even some of her long-standing customers from Toorak were happy to make the trip to Hawthorn. Her nocturnal activities with Rory had borne fruit and they now had two children: Emma who was seven and Andrew who was three. She made a point of speaking to them in French three days a week so that they would grow up bilingual. Some of Rory's male friends had commiserated with him when the first child was a girl, assuming he would be wanting a successor in the Richmond football team at some future time. But he explained that he very much welcomed the opportunity to bring up a little girl to be totally independent and to expect fully equal treatment wherever she went. Sometimes men found his feminist position tiresome, but he always replied that for centuries, if not millennia, man had had the dominant and privileged position, so it was about time men recognised that they were only half of our society, and that it was now time for the other half to have full and equal access to all areas of the economy and society. He recommended that they should stop their belief that women's role was only in the bedroom and the kitchen; that at parties they should stop congregating in the doorways just talking amongst themselves about cars and football; that they should accept that women have excellent brains with interests which extended beyond cars and football into a variety of social, cultural, and political issues. Rory now had a job with one of the commercial radio stations commenting on the football, so together with his salary as a member of the state parliament and Lorraine's success with her hairdressing salon they were financially secure, and able to shift from their cottage into a gracious Victorian villa around the corner in Lisson Grove.

Samuel had finished his law degree and had been establishing a successful practice as a barrister in the Victorian courts. Rory had been to watch him play for the University football team and asked him if he would like to come to a Richmond training session and perhaps he could get a place in the Richmond reserve team. Samuel was delighted with his opportunity to play in the major league, even if it was in the reserve team. Rory even arranged that in one match, when Richmond was playing one of the lower placed teams in the premier league, Samuel could be named as a substitution. Peter Wood agreed that if they were well ahead at half-time he would come off and allow Samuel to take his place. All of Samuel's family came to the match to cheer Samuel on, even if he was playing against their own team: St Kilda.

Because of the equal opportunities legislation which Vida Goldstein had ensured was passed through the various state legislatures, there was quite a lot of litigation so Samuel became a leading authority in this area of law. Samuel and Golda had two daughters: Hannah and Judith. They had bought a house in Kew, a suburb now becoming popular with the Jewish community.

Claudette's father had returned safely from the battlefield and was delighted to hear that she was involved with one of the Australian soldiers who had taken part in the Christmas truce, which had initiated the peace seeking process. When she told him that she had been the bridesmaid at Lorraine and Rory's wedding he was even more excited because he had heard about Rory's instrumental role in the peace process. She told him that Louis had been one of the best players in the match which had taken place between the Australians and the Germans. Claudette and Louis agonised over the future, about whether it should be in Australia or France. Claudette explained that because of her mother's unfortunate early death and the fact that she was the oldest girl in the family she had long been responsible for playing the domestic role in her father's house and she was uneasy about leaving him "as he works such long hours." Louis wasn't sure about how, as a foreigner, he would go about getting employment in France. Father came to the rescue: "What do you know about cars, how they work and how to repair them?"

"That's my business and, as Claudette has just told you, I work long hours so I could do with an assistant." Louis replied that technical subjects were the ones he had excelled in at school and he was sure he could learn quite quickly how to repair a car. So it was resolved that Claudette and Louis would be married in the local village church and that Louis would learn to be a car mechanic. Louis asked that the wedding be delayed until his mother could be present, as she would be so excited that he was going to marry a French girl.

Colonel Monash had been appointed as the Vice Chancellor of the University of Melbourne and had been promoted, so he was now General Monash. He enthusiastically supported the new policy that Australia should just have a small standing volunteer army whose role was purely for the defence of Australia and not engage in foreign expeditions in the defence of other countries. Most Australians were aware of Louise Mack's report of the dealings between the Australian ambassador to France and the French president, so there was overwhelming support for this policy of never again sending Australian troops to fight in foreign fields.

Chapter Ten

Celebrations

MAJOR celebrations were planned to mark the 10th anniversary of the peace settlement. They were to begin with a remembrance ceremony at Ypres. Pierre, Fritz, Wilhelm and Angus were close at hand, but Rory and Samuel were at the other end of the world. The company on whose liner Lorraine had first travelled to Britain had made a lot of money transporting troops to and from Europe, so they were happy to offer free passage to Rory, Samuel and their families. The Earl and Countess of Holborn and Golda's parents were at Waterloo station to meet them and welcome them back to London. The Earl invited the four of them for dinner in Belgravia when they got back from the French celebrations and he explained to Lorraine that he had a little surprise for her when she came to visit. The Countess rolled her eyes and Rory wondered what was going on. There was a courtesy car from the Ritz awaiting them, and the two families were whisked off to spend the night there before they set off for France the next day. The four children had great fun running around Green Park as they have been confined to the ship for five weeks. They were taken over to see Buckingham Palace and had it explained to them that, when they returned from France, their parents would be going there one day to have lunch with the King and Queen.

When they went down for dinner in the evening with Golda's parents they recognised the sommelier. He didn't bother to bring the wine list; instead he just said to Lorraine, "I assume Madam would just like the Chablis and Volnay as usual?" She was delighted to tell him that, since she had last seen him, she had visited both of those estates and sampled some of the finest vintages. Next morning they were up early to catch the train to Dover followed by the ferry to Calais. Claudette and Louis were there to meet them accompanied by Louis' mother, Simone, and Claudette's father, Jacques. Louis explained that they had bought two cars to transport them to Ypres. Louis was now a fully qualified car mechanic and he and Jacques had the biggest car dealership in Pas de Calais. A new 24 hour car race had recently been established in Le Mans and he and Jacques had competed in it to raise the profile of the car dealership. They hadn't won but they were well placed so they now had lots of potential customers coming into their showroom.

Lorraine suggested that they visit a local café for a late French breakfast before they set off for Ypres. The four children were excited to have this first experience of French life, and Emma and Andrew were fascinated to listen to everyone in the café speaking the other language which their mother was teaching them. Emma decided to try her French out so, when the waitress returned with a pile of pain au chocolat and coffee for the adults, she explained to her that this was the very first time she had been in France. The waitress complimented her on her French and said she must have had a very good teacher. Louis explained to Rory about his new passion for motor racing and that he played as a left back for the local soccer team. The four children got in one car with Louis and Claudette, the four adults in the other car with Jacques and Simone. Simone explained that she had come to stay for a couple of months so she could attend the wedding of Louis and Claudette and had been so excited to be in France for the first time. She had found Jacques to be so different from Australian men and after a few weeks he has proposed to her. "We are both widowed; I have come to love you and I don't see why it's only our children who should be having fun, so please marry me." She hadn't hesitated to accept his proposal.

When they arrived at the famous war memorial in Ypres, there was a large contingent of Accrington Pals and Northern Highlanders. Graham Blakey and Angus MacDonald immediately came over to welcome them, but most impressive was Fergus Buchanan in his Buchanan tartan kilt. He had with him a woman who they immediately recognised as Madame from the café behind the front line. The children had never before seen a man in a kilt so Fergus had to explain to them that it was traditional dress for a Scotsman and something they always wore when they went into battle. The memorial listed the names of the dead from both sides of the battle, so many were looking for the names of friends or relatives who had been lost in the battle. The memorial service included poems which had been written by a couple of famous English poets. It finished with a bugler playing the Last Post. Next Madame invited them back to "Café des Australians" to drink some plonk. Claudette gave Louis a big hug and Lorraine explained to her children why it was called plonk, which made Emma giggle. When they got there, Madame disappeared into the cellar and came up with several bottles of wine. Most were from Muscadet but she did bring up two bottles of vin ordinaire "just in case you want to relive your wartime experience". The four children enjoyed the conviviality of the occasion, which was so different to anything they had ever experienced in Melbourne. Emma had great fun practising her French on the locals. They stayed the night at a little hotel in the village and when the proprietor realised that these were the families of Rory and Samuel, of peacemaker fame, he refused to accept any payment for the accommodation. He explained that if it hadn't been for them this hotel might be a German Gasthaus and goodness knows where he would be.

Next morning they set off for the war cemeteries which contained the remains of Australian, British, French and German troops. Rory found Alan Wright's grave and Louis, Lorraine and Rory stood around it crying. When Rory had been given the Freedom of the City of Richmond he had been given an enamel insignia to the effect that he was a Freeman of the City. He had brought it with him together with some cement fixing solution and with Louis' assistance he attached it to the cross bearing Alan's name. Emma had rarely seen her father cry, so she asked Lorraine what was going on, and it was explained to her that Alan was a teammate of Rory and Louis who had been killed in the war. It suddenly dawned on her for the first time that Rory could have been killed in that war and she wouldn't be here. They now set off in the two cars for Nancy, where major celebrations were planned. Since Nancy had been chosen by the gang of six for the location for the peace talks, it had come to worldwide attention, and it was now a major tourist destination, especially for those who loved the art nouveau style. The town's business folk, and in particular the hotels and restaurants, were very grateful to the gang of six for the prosperity they had enjoyed for the last 10 years.

When Lorraine and Rory walked into the Grand Hotel de la Reine she reminded the desk staff that 10 years ago she had promised to be back. Rory explained to his children that they were now in Lorraine and would be staying here for a few days for the celebrations. Emma replied that eight years ago she had actually spent several months living in Lorraine. Andrew was puzzled by what his precocious sister had said as he knew she was only seven. The twelve of them now set off for Brasserie Excelsior where a special table had been arranged for them. The four children were stunned by it as they had never seen anything so beautiful in Melbourne. Some of the locals remembered Lorraine and Rory from their honeymoon and came up to acknowledge Rory, so he introduced them all to Samuel and explained that he had been equally instrumental in the peace process, so lots of the locals insisted on coming up to shake the hands of Rory and Samuel and to kiss Lorraine and Golda on the cheek. The children were most amused to see their mothers being kissed by lots of strange men.

After a delicious dinner they returned to Place Stanislas which was crowded with a merrymaking throng. Fireworks were being set off from a nearby park and a stage had been set up in the middle of the Place and a brass band was playing Le Marseille, God save the King and Waltzing Matilda. The cafés in the Place were busy serving glasses of petit chablis.

They spent the next days exploring the art nouveau delights of Nancy and the evenings dining in Brasserie Excelsior and carousing in Place Stanislas. Simone was very excited at being able to experience France in a way that she had missed out on all her life, and Claudette, who had never been to Nancy before, marvelled at the diversity of her country. The Mayor of Nancy had taken to the stage in the Place and introduced Rory and Samuel to the crowd. He said that he intended to recommend to the French government that they be awarded the Legion d'Honneur. Rory thanked the Mayor but informed him that they would have to decline such an honour because of the way in which the customs union, of which France was a member, had treated Australian trade. It was rare for anyone to decline the Legion d'Honneur, so Rory explained to him what had happened. Inevitably the Mayor was appalled to hear how such a valuable ally had been treated and never again would he vote for that French President or his political party.

Meanwhile there were also celebrations taking place in Paris, and Olga and Madeleine had invited Marie Curie, Pierre and Graham to dinner at La Tour d'Argent. Olga re-counted the inroads which women had made into the French economy and society in the last 10 years. The chief executive of the Bank of France was a woman, as was the chief executive of the major French car manufacturer. Women now drove the Metro trains and taxis in Paris. Lyon's women's soccer team was one of the very best in the world. As Graham had instigated this movement for female equality by recommending Emmeline Pankhurst as a member of the peace negotiations, he was well esteemed by the feminist movement and Olga had recommended him to be awarded the Legion d'Honneur. "Golly" said Graham, "I'll be Graham Blakey MP, CBE, LH, it's such a pity that my father is not here to see it."

When the Hunters and Harcourts left Nancy they headed south into Burgundy as it had been arranged that they should visit several villages to participate in the 10th anniversary of peace. During the last decade Lorraine had scoured the Melbourne bookstores for books on art and French wine. She had learnt that one of the most delicious and expensive French wines came from a small village in Burgundy called Vosne Romanée. She had asked if that village could be put on their itinerary. When they arrived Lorraine spoke to the vintners who were there to greet them. She told them that she had vintner friends in both Chablis and Volnay and that they were also visiting those villages to celebrate the 10th anniversary of the peace settlement. Like so many in Northern France the vintners of Vosne Romanée had been in great fear for their future if the Germans had been victorious in the war, so they ensured that a lady, who obviously was well connected with the producers of Burgundy wine, was able to sample some of their best vintages. It was even more exceptional than what she had believed from her books. Lorraine thanked the vintners profusely and confirmed that it would have been a great tragedy if the vines had fallen into German hands. When they climbed into the car, Lorraine told them how much the wine they had been drinking would cost if it had been bought in a shop or restaurant. Even Jacques was surprised and Samuel knew that his father would be incredulous, and concerned to know if Samuel had been profligate enough to buy a bottle.

They moved on to Chablis which was decked out in Tricolors and a brass band was playing next to two pedestals. After the Mayor had performed his welcoming ceremony, Lorraine's vintner friends explained that a large open air meal had been organised so that the townsfolk would have the opportunity to meet Rory and Samuel. As usual the children ran around enjoying the foreign nature of the village and wanted to know why their fathers' names were engraved on one of the pedestals in the middle of the town. The vintners told Lorraine that they had found some appropriate land for a vineyard in the Yarra valley and would shortly be coming out to Australia to plant some Pinot Noir vines. Lorraine explained that when the Yarra reached the city it was almost at the bottom of her street and that they must come to visit her so that she could repay their generous hospitality. After spending the night in Chablis they moved on to Volnay where there was a repeat performance and the children were becoming even more curious about their fathers' name being engraved on a pedestal. The following morning Louis and Jacques drove them to Calais so that they could get the ferry and train back to London. Louis and Simone assured them that they very much enjoyed their life in France and didn't really miss Richmond.

When they arrived back at the Ritz there was a letter awaiting them from Maynard Keynes. It was an invitation for them to spend an evening at his house in Gordon Square, Bloomsbury. In it he explained that Virginia Woolf would like to meet the two men who had initiated the peace process, which had then led to so much feminist success. He added that Emmeline Pankhurst and Millicent Fawcett would be present. Graham Blakey had also been invited because he had initiated the nomination of a feminist to the peace negotiating team. Keynes explained he had a new wife, Lydia Lopokova, who was also looking forward to meeting them. There was much excitement at having received such an invitation. Samuel knew of Keynes' reputation in economics and finance and was certain he would go down in history as one of the most significant men of the 20th century; Golda, as a Londoner, knew of the avant-garde reputation of the Bloomsbury set so was very keen to participate in it for an evening; in the pursuit of his interest in feminism Rory had read "A Room of One's Own", so he was excited to meet Virginia Woolf; in addition to her interest in art and French wine Lorraine had a passion for ballet and she knew that Lydia was one of the world's most famous ballerinas. Lorraine replied immediately accepting the kind invitation and asked whether she might bring her young daughter Emma who was attending ballet school and would love to meet a real ballerina.

Next morning Golda's mother arrived to take the children off to visit the Natural History Museum and the four adults strolled across Green Park to have lunch at the Palace. King George was aware of Lorraine's interest in fine French wine so he had arranged for some excellent Bordeaux vintages to be served, to contrast with the Burgundy wine which she was accustomed to. Queen Mary asked what the children were doing today and, as she had never met a male feminist before, she was keen to ask Rory about his views and what it was like to be coaching a female football team. King George asked if they could tell him why Australia had voted to be a republic rather than remain a Dominion in the British Empire. Samuel explained that there were several reasons: one was Australian soldiers' resentment at the arrogance and condescension of British officers; another was the fact that Australia had a large Irish catholic population which resented British behaviour in Ireland and the third was that the Scottish had a long resented rule from Westminster and this had carried over when they emigrated to Australia; the fourth was that many Australian women were disgusted at the way Britain had treated its suffragettes. It did not help that the Governor General was usually some minor English aristocrat rather than an Australian. The King obviously had a lot to discuss the next time his Prime Minister had an audience with him. When they were leaving, the King said that it was one of his most pleasant duties to lunch with members of the Order of Merit and he hoped it would not be another 10 years before he met them all again.

They hurried back across Green Park because it was Friday and they were all going to Golders Green for dinner with Golda's parents. The parents were very pleased to hear Golda say that Jews were well integrated into Australian society and that incidents of anti-Semitism were very rare. Perhaps because it was a country newly settled, mainly by Irish and Scottish people, so did not have a history of Jewish antagonism like they had in Russia and parts of Europe. Hannah and Judith had never visited their grandparents' house before, so it was a special occasion for them. When Rory explained that Samuel had played for his team in a match against the team which was much favoured by the Melbourne Jewish community everyone was amused. Golda's father said it was as if he had played for Arsenal against Tottenham Hotspur.

The next day they took the children to the Tower of London and Samuel explained to them its significance in British history. In the evening Golda's mother came to babysit so that the four adults could go off to Belgravia to fulfil the Earl's invitation. Lorraine introduced Samuel and Golda to the Earl and Countess and the Countess explained that her son, the Major, was present and, as previously, she had invited the Australian High Commissioner and those of her friends who were interested in feminist issues. The Countess told Lorraine that, as she probably had expected, she had been placed next to the Earl at dinner. He came over and told Lorraine that there was something in his study that he would like to show her. It was a beautiful Laurencin painting of two Spanish Senoritas with a pink fan.

The Major was seated next to Samuel and set about thanking him for his role in the peace process, as he had done ten years previously when he had met Rory. The ladies present were keen to know if Rory had been able to maintain his feminist position in a country with such a machismo reputation. He confirmed that he had never wavered in his feminist beliefs and, as he was now a member of the State Parliament, he did all he could to support Vida Goldstein in her role as Minister for Women in the Federal Parliament. The ladies were surprised that not only did women play Australian football but that Rory was the coach of one of the leading clubs.

The Earl asked Lorraine about Australian painters and she told him that she very much liked the works of Margaret Preston, the artist who had designed the new Australian flag. She added that before they returned to Australia they were visiting Madrid, as she wanted to see the works of Joaquin Sorolla. He was a Spanish impressionist who painted beautiful pictures of women in flowing robes walking on the beach and many beautiful portraits of his wife Clothilde. One of her favourites was Clothilde lying in bed with her newborn baby beside her. Lorraine added that obviously they would also visit the Prado while they were in Madrid as she also very much admired the work of Goya. The Earl replied that he and the Countess usually spent their holidays in Scotland or France, but now he must persuade her to take a Spanish holiday for the first time and visit Madrid. When desert was served he informed Lorraine that he had a surprise for her:

as she was such an aficionado of modern painting he had specified in his will that she was to have the Laurencin. His wife and son knew of this and totally approved. Obviously Lorraine was overjoyed at the prospect of one day owning a Laurencin, so she thanked the Earl profusely and said she hoped it would be many years before she received it She had brought her camera and had a photo of herself taken alongside the Laurencin. When they were leaving Lorraine kissed the Earl on the cheek and thanked him again.

The next evening Golda's mother was on duty again as babysitter, and she was having great fun spending time with her two granddaughters. The four parents and Emma were off to the Bloomsbury soirée. Maynard welcomed them and introduced them all around. Virginia immediately approached Rory to ask how he, as an Australian man, had become interested in feminism as she had heard that, like America, Australia had a very machismo culture. He explained that the person responsible for opening his eyes to the disparity of treatment between men and women was Vida Goldstein who had come to visit his wife before their wedding. Vida was now Minister for Women in the Federal Government and he, as a member of the State Parliament, did everything he could to support her endeavours. He added that, to further his understanding of feminism, he had read the Subjection of Women and her own book A Room of One's Own.

Emmeline and Millicent were equally fascinated to understand Graham's motivation in nominating a feminist for the peace negotiating team. He explained that it was a natural progression of his father's activity as a Chartist pressing for full adult male franchise. Virginia suggested that it would be worthwhile to review the progress of feminism in the four countries over the last 10 years and begin to plan what further progress was needed in the next decade. Emmeline was in regular contact with the German and French feminists and Rory was conversant with what was happening in Australia, so Virginia thought that the current gathering was well placed to make such a review. All four countries had made major progress with respect to women's health with contraceptive advice being widely available and abortion having been legalised, although there had been some difficulties in Australia because of its federal structure. Divorce law was now reformed so that "the irretrievable breakdown of the marriage", rather than some marital crime, was the criterion for the dissolution of marriage.

There had been considerable success in opening up employment to women so that they now had access to jobs in law, medicine and the skilled trades. The women were fascinated to hear from Rory that it was a militant male trade unionist who had first ensured that women in Australia must get equal pay for equal work. All four countries now had women playing sport which previously had been reserved for men. In athletics women were no longer confined to the sprints, but also raced over the middle distance events and there was talk of them running the marathon. There were women members of all four Parliaments and their Cabinets. But it was only in Germany that women occupied the most senior Cabinet positions, where Rosa was Minister for Finance and Clara was Minister for Defence. None of the four countries had a female Prime Minister or female Foreign Minister. There were no female surgeons or judges or engineers and there were very few females with senior positions in finance. Women dominated the string sections of orchestras but there were no female conductors. The captains of the ocean liners which plied the oceans of the world were always male.

Virginia summed up: there had been considerable progress over the past decade but there was still some way to go to establish full sexual equality in employment. Experienced women in parliament must be encouraged to lobby for senior Cabinet posts and female junior doctors encouraged to pursue a career in surgery. The Lord Chancellor needs to recognise the ability of female barristers and ensure that some are appointed to the bench. In Britain the Bank of England must be pressed to appoint at least one woman to its advisory body, in order to demonstrate to the City of London that women have the intellectual attributes to shine in economics and finance, as Rosa had done in Germany and in world finance bodies. Maynard explained that he had a young female colleague at Cambridge called Jean Robinson who would overwhelm them with her intellect and forthrightness. During rest sections of rehearsals leading female violinists should be encouraged to pick up the baton and start conducting the orchestra, so as to demonstrate they had that talent. "If we meet in 10 years' time, I expect to hear that there is at least one female prime minister, many female surgeons and anaesthetists, several senior executives of major finance institutions and women as principal conductors of some of the worlds leading orchestras," said Virginia.

Meanwhile Emma had been sitting on Lydia's knee and being told about the hard life that a ballerina led. Lydia said that she wished she had a little girl of her own just like Emma and would Emma like to come later in the week when she was going to be dancing Princess Aurora in The Sleeping Beauty? Naturally Lorraine was interested to talk to the two artists present, Vanessa Bell and Duncan

Grant, and she explained to them why they were travelling to Madrid before they returned to Australia. Lorraine had brought her camera so she took a photo of Emma sitting on Lydia's knee and she asked Virginia, Emmeline and Millicent if they would mind standing together, so that she could photograph Emma standing in front of them. When she grew older they would be photographs she would treasure.

Two days later, when they came down for breakfast, there was an envelope with eight tickets and an invitation from Lydia to watch her dance Princess Aurora that evening at the Coliseum. The five female members were very excited, and Rory said that he had read that male ballet dancers were the fittest of all sportsmen so he was very interested to watch ballet. When Lydia performed the fouettés they were overwhelmed at how spectacular her performance was. Afterwards they were invited backstage to see her and the five female members of the contingent surrounded her to acclaim the elegance of her performance. Rory was talking to her partner and asked him what fitness regime he had to enable him to perform such a demanding role.

When their London stay came to an end there were tearful farewells for Golda's family at Victoria station. They stayed overnight in Paris and went to Les Deux Magots for dinner. The Harcourt family were most impressed with Lorraine's fluency in French, so Hannah and Judith were resolved to concentrate hard in French lessons, so that they might emulate her in the future. Next morning they were all up early to catch the train to Madrid. Eating in the dining car and watching the countryside slide by was quite a novelty for the children. They wanted to know why they had to change from a French train into a Spanish train at a town called Irun. Samuel explained that France and

Spain had different train gauges, which referred to the distance between the rails, so French trains could not travel on Spanish railways and vice versa. He explained that it was exactly the same if you travel by train from Melbourne to Sydney, as the two states had different gauges and in this case you had to change trains at a town called Albury. Because she knew she was coming to Madrid, Lorraine had spent some time learning Spanish, and whilst not aspiring to be as fluent as she was in French, she knew that speaking some basic Spanish would make life in Madrid easier.

When they arrived at Atocha station in Madrid Lorraine arranged for them to get two taxis for their journey to the hotel. They were staying at a hotel close to the Plaza Mayor, which she had read was a magnificent large square in the middle of Madrid. After unpacking their luggage they strolled over to the Plaza and were staggered by its size and beauty. There was nothing like it in either London or Paris. It was full of Spaniards sitting in outdoor cafés drinking wine. They wandered around the perimeter of the square and when they came to one corner there was a set of steps leading down to the streets of Old Madrid so they descended and when they got to the bottom there were waiters dressed as pirates handing out menus for the restaurant. Naturally the children were fascinated and they asked if they could eat there that evening. Lorraine asked a waiter if they could have a table for eight people and the pirates replied certainly, but they could not come until 9 o'clock as that was the earliest that Madrileños ate. As they had a long time to wait they strolled further down the street and suddenly Samuel became quite excited as they came upon a restaurant called Botins. Samuel was a great fan of Ernest Hemingway and he knew that this was his favourite restaurant and was mentioned in one of his novels. Lorraine had read in a guidebook that it was allegedly the oldest restaurant in the world and that in his youth Goya had worked there as a waiter. Lorraine went inside and said she would like to book a table for eight tomorrow evening and once again she was told not to come before nine.

When 9 o'clock came they went back to the restaurant where the "pirates" were busy setting out menus, which were in both Spanish and English. Samuel's eyes immediately lit on a dish called "squid in its own ink". This was another of Hemingway's favourites so he immediately decided to order it. The children didn't fancy eating anything cooked in ink, and chose the chicken, but the other adults decided to try it, which is something they knew Peter Wood certainly would do if he were here. To begin the meal Lorraine suggested that they could try a famous Spanish soup called gazpacho. It was a cold soup made with tomatoes, cucumbers, peppers and olive oil. She ordered it for eight people and when it came the waiter had a dish divided into four which contained chopped up cucumber, bread cubes, chopped up peppers, and chopped up spring onions. He asked each guest which of these they would like added to their soup. Lorraine knew that the most famous Spanish wine area was called Rioja and she knew that when Bordeaux wine had been decimated by phylloxera it was wine from this area that the French substituted, so that is what she chose to order. It was very late for the children when they returned to their hotel so the following morning they slept late. After a leisurely breakfast at a café in the Plaza they jumped into taxis to take them to Sorollo's house, which was now set up as a museum to his memory. When they entered the garden Lorraine immediately recognised it from one of his famous paintings. Inside there were several paintings of Clothilde, including the one of her in bed with her newborn baby. The three girls all wanted to know if it was usual practice for mothers to have babies in bed with them, as they had only ever seen them in their own crib. They all knew that they were destined for motherhood some day, so were interested to know all about it. The painting which the girls really liked was one of some girls skipping around a pond.

They arrived at Botins at 9 o'clock and found a table of eight set up for them. Samuel knew that the thing to order here was roast suckling pig so everyone agreed to have it and, as they had enjoyed the gazpacho the previous evening they decided to begin with it. The waiter told Lorraine that one of the most famous wines from Rioja was Marques de Murrieta, so she ordered it. After they had finished the gazpacho the waiter came in with two large platters to display the roast piglets before he cut them up to serve. The children were alarmed to see the whole little piglet displayed in its roasted state, but it was explained to them that most of us are omnivores and when they enjoy those lamb chops back in Melbourne they had come from those little white woolly things they had seen running around fields in the countryside. The waiter returned with eight plates of roast piglet, which was delicious, especially as it was accompanied by an outstanding wine. Samuel said that he had been led to believe that France was the most famous country for its cuisine, but after two meals in Spain he now considered that it was a strong rival to France.

Colonel Monash, who now was General Sir John Monash, was also in Europe for the 10th anniversary of the peace. In particular he had come to thank the Scandinavians and the Spanish for their participation in the peace process, and their ongoing responsibility for ensuring there was no clandestine production of armaments in either France or Germany. There was not much need to worry about Germany, as Clara was zealous in ensuring that its military had no offensive philosophy or capacity. Sir John was currently in Madrid to thank the Spanish military for their invaluable contribution to the peace process and to check if they had any difficulty in their investigative role. Because of the history of conflict with France there had been minor difficulties, but they had been easily resolved by involving the officers from Scandinavia.

Rory and Samuel had arranged to meet up with Sir John and his wife Hannah in Madrid. They decided to have lunch at an outdoor café in the Plaza Mayor so that the children would be able to run around. Most chose either a Spanish omelette or fried anchovies or "judias con jamon", which Lorraine explained was green beans with ham. She also told them that, as there was six of them present the Spanish word for Jew was exactly the same as the Spanish word for green bean. This caused much amusement and Golda switched her order from a tortilla to the judias, saying that she hoped they tasted as good as Samuel. This prompted him also to change his order to the judias, " to check if they tasted like Golda". The salad was made from chopped up avocados, peppers, small tomatoes and Spanish onion, so it was very different from the salad that the children were accustomed to in Melbourne which was made of iceberg lettuce and large tough tomatoes. They drank sangria, which was served in a large pitcher and consisted of red wine, a spirit called Triple Seco de Malaga, mineral water, lemon and a little spoonful of sugar.

Sir John said to Samuel that he had spoken to the Dean of the Law School and suggested that Samuel should be appointed as a part-time lecturer to teach this new area of equal opportunity legislation, as he was obviously a leading member of the Victorian bar in that field. Samuel was delighted to accept and revealed that he was keen that the criteria be extended to include race, "so that we can start to redress the harm and injustice which the European invaders have imposed on the indigenous people of Australia." Rory was listening intently and said that when they got back to Melbourne he would consult with Samuel about what legislation he considered necessary to start putting this injustice to rights. Samuel replied that one action which could be taken immediately was to ensure that indigenous children had equal and sympathetic access to education. Not a single Victorian indigenous Australian had matriculated from high school and that was a disgrace. Sir John intervened to say that when an indigenous Australian did matriculate he would ensure that there was a scholarship which offered a free place and a living allowance to attend the University of Melbourne.

The three men agreed that, if Australia were to go ahead with the large-scale immigration policy, which was being discussed by the federal government, Spain would be an excellent place to start. Spaniards were very friendly and gregarious people and they obviously knew how to produce excellent fruit, vegetables, piglets, rice and wine so they would contribute immensely to the diversity of Australian life. Rory said that if the federal government agreed with such a policy he would press the State Government to encourage the new immigrants to settle in an inner Melbourne suburb which was in need of refurbishment, as he knew that the Spaniards would soon enliven it.

After lunch they headed for the Prado, in particular to see the Goyas. The three men, who were veterans of military conflict, were all horrified by Goya's painting "The 3rd of May 1808". It showed a Spanish freedom fighter being summarily executed by French troops. Lorraine set off to find the two Majas: clothed and naked. They were both very beautiful paintings, but Golda and Lorraine both inevitably noted the interest which their husbands took in the naked Maja. Goya's famous black paintings were kept together in a separate room and mainly depicted very old people in a decrepit state; the most horrific was one of Satan devouring his own son. They decided to eat again at the "Pirates" and next morning set off on the train to Barcelona. The boat to Naples left a day later so there was time to see some of Barcelona's spectacular buildings. They started with Gaudi's Casa Batllo, which the children decided was like the house in the fairytale Hansel and Gretel. Next they moved on to the Palau de la Musica Catalana which was also fantastical. Finally they visited the very unfinished cathedral, La Sagrada Familia. Lorraine had read that there was a famous restaurant called The Four Cats, so they set off there for their final dinner in Spain. Roast kid was on the menu so Lorraine quickly explained to the children that this referred to a baby goat, not one of them. Next morning they sailed across the Mediterranean to Naples and the boat which was taking them back to Port Melbourne.

When they arrived home in Hawthorn Lorraine and Rory found, amongst their mail, a letter from the French vintners telling them that they had found an excellent location for a vineyard in a little town called Dixons Creek. They were welcome to visit them one weekend when they returned from Europe.

Rory immediately set about organising a meeting with Samuel and Vida Goldstein to discuss action to improve access to education and employment of indigenous

Australians. The only indigenous Australian who Rory knew was a footballer who played for a team in an associated league, so he attended their next match and called upon him in the changing room afterwards. Rory explained the project and invited Douglas to take part, which he did enthusiastically. The following week the four met to discuss the action necessary to achieve racial equality in Australia. Samuel offered to draft legislation making racial discrimination in education, employment and personal services illegal. Vida said that currently she was Minister for Women but she would press for that to be changed to Minister for Equality. In the interim she could still intervene because 50% of indigenous Australians obviously were women, so she could begin action aimed at ensuring that they were treated exactly like the white European population. Douglas pointed out that, in Victoria, there were indigenous Australian settlements in Lake Tyers, Benalla and Terang, so they were obvious places to begin investigating schooling. Rory explained that he would speak to the Minister for Education and get his authority to convene a meeting of school inspectors to discuss this issue, and also permission to visit schools in those three areas.

Once the four started to take action it inevitably leaked out to the press, and one of the tabloids took a predictably offensive racist line. It asserted that indigenous Australians were an inferior race who were lazy, untrustworthy and addicted to alcohol. Samuel was outraged, as it reminded him of the history of anti-Semitism of which he was aware. He announced that the legislation which he was recommending would now be extended to include making incitement to racial hatred a criminal offence. This led to the inevitable response that he was intending to curb freedom of speech.

When he met with the school inspectors Rory invited Douglas to accompany him. He immediately asked the school inspectors how come no indigenous Australian had successfully completed secondary school and passed the matriculation examination. In reply it was asserted that these students lacked the motivation and perseverance for academic success. Rory said that he and Douglas would accompany the senior inspector to Lake Tyers, so that he could check whether school principals concurred with this assessment. On the whole, the school principals did support the views of the inspector, but there was one, Donald Waters, who had a more thoughtful and sympathetic interpretation of the situation. He said that they came from a culture where it was essential to learn about the land and how to live off it; that some subjects such as British history and algebra were alien to them. He did not doubt that they have the intellectual capacity to master such subjects, but that they needed to be introduced to them thoughtfully. He recommended that when they first started school they be taught together in small groups by teachers specially trained to understand their different cultural background. In some subjects such as art and physical education they should be integrated with the white European students, as indigenous Australians excelled in these areas, and we should not give any impression that they were being segregated in the school. Schools sports teams, drama productions, singing and musical activities should all be integrated. As they progressed through the school, and particularly into the secondary school, they should progressively be integrated into normal classes but be given extra support where necessary. This sounded like a sensible policy to Rory, but he asked Douglas to check with the elders in the Victorian group of indigenous Australians whether they found this an acceptable approach.

The legislation which Samuel had drafted successfully passed through the Victorian Parliament, and Vida acted to give it support at federal level and pressed the other state governments to follow the lead given by Victoria. Douglas confirmed that the elders were agreeable to Donald's suggestions, so Donald was transferred to the Melbourne Teacher's College to set about training a cohort of students to fulfil this new role. Rory realised that it would be several years before this new initiative bore any fruit, but in the interim he intended to visit the schools on a regular basis and consult with Donald about progress.

Meanwhile Lorraine, Rory and the children had made the short journey to Dixons Creek to see the progress which their vintner friends had made in establishing their vineyard. They had searched extensively in Victoria and decided that the "terroir" here in Dixons Creek would be ideal for the Pinot Noir grape they wanted to plant. Because of the opposing seasons in the northern and southern hemisphere they were planning to divide their lives in future between Burgundy and Dixons Creek. Emma, in particular, was quite excited to hear this as it meant that for half the year she would be able to practise her French with real French people.

Addendum

1929

ONE day a crate was delivered to their house in Lisson Grove. It was addressed to Lorraine and the sender was noted as the Earl of Holborn. Lorraine was very excited as she knew what it was and asked Rory to help her unpack it very carefully. He was confused because it was his understanding that she would only receive the painting when the Earl was dead. She explained that his son, the Major whom he had met, would automatically assume the title of Earl on his father's death, so it was this new Earl who had sent the painting. When they opened it she was in for a very big surprise: the crate contained Marie Laurencin's painting of the two Spanish señoritas with a pink fan, but it also contained a portrait of Clothilde by her husband, Joaquin Sorolla. There was a letter from the new Earl explaining that his parents had travelled to Madrid soon after their last meeting with Lorraine, and that the Earl had much appreciated the paintings of Sorolla and had been grateful to Lorraine for drawing this artist to his attention, so he had naturally added this painting of Clothilde to his bequest.

Lorraine had the paintings hanged in pride of place in their living room and set about inviting all her friends to view them. Lady Bailey, who was quite an aficionado, confessed that she had not known of the work of either of these artists, but recognised immediately that they were both extremely talented, and on her next trip to Europe she would certainly be seeking their work out in the appropriate galleries. She added that the Director of the Victorian State Art Gallery was a friend of hers, and would Lorraine mind if she informed him that Lorraine possessed these two paintings, as she was sure he would like to see them?

The Director called on Lorraine the next week and said that he knew of both these artists but never before had seen any of their paintings. He was delighted to see a work by each of them for the first time, and he wondered if Lorraine would agree to them being displayed in the State Gallery for a month, so that the general public would have the opportunity to view them. He assured her that maximum care would be taken of them and there would be a security guard always present to protect them. Lorraine was always conscious of the distance she had travelled from her humble backgrounds in a small Richmond cottage and was certainly happy to share her good fortune with others, so immediately agreed to his request.

She had a romantic, compassionate, feminist husband, two energetic inquisitive children, and amongst her friends were some liberal Jews, eminent French Vintners, and famous feminists such as Vida Goldstein. She could look forward to her children growing up, her husband progressing in his political career, regular Friday evening dinners with the Harcourts, and spending time in summer and autumn in Dixons Creek with her French friends.